LOST AND MISUNDERSTOOD

Lost and Misunderstood
Edited by Radhika Menon
Print Edition

First Printed & Published in India in 2021
Inkfeathers Publishing, New Delhi 110095

Copyright © Inkfeathers Publishing, 2021
Cover Design © 2020 Inkfeathers Publishing
Cover Image © S. Hermann & F. Richter from Pixabay

All rights reserved.

ISBN 978-81-949324-1-3

www.inkfeathers.com

LOST AND MISUNDERSTOOD

edited & compiled by

RADHIKA MENON

DISCLAIMER

The anthology "Lost and Misunderstood" is a collection of stories by 27 authors who belong to different parts of the globe. The anthology editor and the publisher have edited the content provided by the co-authors to enhance the experience for readers and make it free of plagiarism as much as possible. All the stories published in this anthology are a work of fiction. Unless otherwise indicated, all the names, characters, objects, businesses, places, events, incidents- whether physical/non-physical, real/unreal, tangible/ intangible in whatsoever description used in this book are either the product of the author's imagination or used in a fictitious manner. Any resemblance to actual persons, objects, entities, living or dead, or actual events is purely coincidental. The stories published in this book are solely owned by their respective authors and are no way intended to hurt anyone's religious, political, spiritual, brand, personal or fanatic beliefs and/or faith, whatsoever. In case, any sort of plagiarism is detected in the stories within this anthology or in case of any complaints or grievances or objections, neither the anthology editor, nor the publisher are to be held responsible for any such claims. The author(s) who holds the rights to the story, shall be held responsible, whatsoever.

CO-AUTHORED BY

Ruchka Gulati ~ Shreya Shenoy ~ Mayuri Kashyap ~ Aaqilah A J ~ Aarti Shahdadpuri ~ Ravgun Kaur ~ Amritha Suryakumar ~ Tipston Rubus ~ Tulsi Nambiar ~ Uma Bokil ~ Radhika Menon ~ Rukma Anil ~ Sanjana Varma ~ Lalitha Srinivas ~ Pritha Shyam ~ Sandhra Sunil ~ Manoj Vaz ~ Shrey Sharma ~ Ar. Jerin Jo Thomas ~ Debajit Deb ~ Kanchan Hiranandani ~ J. Jerome ~ Kavya Mithran ~ Arijit Roy ~ Snehal Agarwal ~ Sumeet Doondani ~ C.L. Williams

CONTENTS

ABOUT THE EDITOR

RADHIKA MENON

Armed with an optimistic perspective on life, Radhika Menon, a passionate poet, has always fought her demons through words. Experienced in the vague nuances of life, she brings you an iconoclastic take on traditional antagonists in this debut. Uniquely qualified to compile this work, as she simultaneously works on building young minds as a teacher, and creates raw poems on dark themes she encounters, this book is a testament to her abilities.

EDITOR'S NOTE

They say that the road to hell is paved with good intentions. Truer words have never been spoken. Life is not black and white. It's fifty shades of grey. Maybe more. Who we see as villains may not have set off to be the evildoers they are perceived to be. There may have been compulsions and misunderstandings that led to them being as lost and misunderstood as they got to be.

Lost and Misunderstood is not just a book, it is a rebellion. It is an amalgamation of the tales of the fallen, the unheard ones, those who were forced to take the path they did by the cruel twists and turns of fate.

They also say, if you want to know a person, ask them to show you their dark side.

What you are holding in your hand is the dark side. Love it or hate it, you just can't ignore it. Happy reading.

Forever lost,
Radhika Menon

1

CHICKEN CUTLET FOR THE SOUL

by Manoj Vaz

I had seen it in one of these magazines," thought Mrs. Iyer, impatiently rummaging through a pile of magazines. "Mutton Rogan Josh, Chicken Hyderabadi, Paneer Pasanda," she read and thought aloud as she flipped the pages, "Where the hell is the wonderful recipe for Soya Mince Cutlet that Mrs. Aasholkar was raving about?"

"Chicken Cutlet..." She paused the incessant flipping of the pages for a couple of seconds and swallowed the sudden involuntary rush of saliva that had formed in her mouth. How she missed her favourite chicken cutlets!

The fact was that Mrs. Iyer was born as Ms. Joyce Pinto. Petite, pretty with long dark brown hair and innocent hazel eyes, she was quite fancied by the boys of St. Stephen's college.

As fate would have it, she met Subramanian Venkateshwaran Iyer at a College Fest and had immediately fallen superlatively in love with his degrees.

Subbu was, at 25 years of age, a Certified C.A., I.C.W.A., C.S., and in the final year of the MBA in Financial Management.

Subbu, who had till then never benefited from feminine attention, was immediately charmed. He was not exactly a stud: 5' 9", dark, skinny, soda glass spectacles and at 25, never been in romantic proximity with any girl.

But he had something that Joyce found the most interesting: appointment letters from 3 foreign banks and 2 mutual funds. Each offering him a fifty lakh plus annual remuneration.

They were married after a brief six-month courtship, which included 2 boring dates and a couple of dozen even more boring telephone conversations. By the end of the period Joyce, an Arts Literature student was beginning to get the hang of calculating the P.E. Ratio and R.O.I of most companies.

Today was their 1st wedding anniversary and Subbu had called his boss, Mr. Sandeep Khosla, home for dinner. Mr. Khosla did not exactly relish the idea of having vegetarian food on a Friday evening, nor did he have an appetite for Subbu's company.

Yet, corporate protocol demanded that he accept the invitation. After all, given Subbu's qualifications, it was only a matter of time that he would be reporting to Subbu and not vice versa.

Subbu was excited too, he had even gone to the extent of buying a bottle of expensive scotch for the occasion.

"I hope Appa doesn't get wind of the fact that I have a bottle of whiskey at home," he prayed.

Subbu's parents were super conservative and ultra-traditional. What's more, they had raised him to be exactly like them. "You have to study hard so that you can do serrrrvice," Iyer Senior would say in his raspy, thickly accented voice.

"Don't even think of starting your own practice... doing business is risky, serrrrvice is best... get a decent fixed salary every month, no ups and no downs."

Subbu had swallowed the gospel and despite getting several good partnership offers, opted to work as a Manager (Portfolio Management) in a multi-national Mutual Fund. Iyer Senior was happy with his son's choice and gloated over it with relatives at every opportunity.

Mrs. Iyer Senior, Subbu's amma too had her fair share of didactic advice, "Perform Nithya puja every morning, recite Gayatri Mantra regularly, be vegetarian and have an arranged marriage with a nice Iyer girl."

Subbu had soured their taste buds when he insisted on marrying Joyce. In the end, they had grudgingly agreed to the blasphemous alliance, but only after Joyce pledged to become a vegetarian and change her name to "Jayanthi".

Back in the kitchen, Joyce, suddenly recollected that the magazine with the recipe was borrowed by the neighbour Mrs. Aasholkar. As it often happens, all she had to do was think of her and the devil rang her doorbell.

"Hi Malini," greeted Joyce. "I hope you have asked Mr. Aasholkar to come home early, it is our first anniversary, I don't want any bad surprises."

Malini smiled, she was 39 for the last 3 years and plump in a voluptuous kind of way "Of course dear, how can we miss your anniversary dinner, I came to ask you if you needed any help with the cooking."

Looking at her low-cut blouse and coquettish mannerisms, Joyce could just not help but wonder if there was any truth in the rumour that Malini was having a torrid affair with their driver, Radheshyam.

"Remember the magazine that had the recipe for Soya Mince Cutlets?" asked Joyce, her thoughts still on Radheshyam, the slick-haired, dark, wiry driver. "I am planning to have the cutlets as a starter along with the drinks because Mr. Khosla is non-vegetarian and well-made soya cutlets almost taste the same as chicken cutlets"

"Almost is not as good as the real thing" teased Malini, "I don't know how you put up with Subbu, if I was in your place, I would have had an affair and run away with someone!"

"Are you?" quipped Joyce, curiosity getting the better of her.

"Am I what, Joyce?" Malini was all innocence.

Joyce hesitated, "Errr... having an affair?"

Butter wouldn't melt in Malini's mouth "Does Vilas think I am having an affair?"

Joyce thought of Vilas Aasholkar... if he knew, hell would have looked like the garden of Eden.

"No, he doesn't!" Joyce replied confidently.

Malini smiled mysteriously and winked "Then I am not," and added, "I better get going, I shall send the magazine with the maid"

Joyce sat down on her comfortable Italian sofa and ruminated over their conversation. She remembered an adage from her English literature book "What the eye doesn't see, the heart doesn't grieve about."

She then thought of Mr. Aasholkar.

Vilas Aasholkar was 48, medium height, stocky, blunt featured and pockmarked. He started off as a lower division clerk in the Income Tax department 25 years ago and progressed to the authoritative position of Joint Commissioner, thanks to the fact that he belonged to a Scheduled Caste according to the Government.

Even as Joint Commissioner, his monthly Rs. 78,684/- salary hardly justified their 3-bedroom apartment in a crème-de-la-crème 28-floor residential tower 'Fountainhead' in hi-profile Lokhandwala Township in Andheri West.

But then the apartment was 'officially' owned by his father-in-law, who 'officially' bought the Rs. 5 Crore 3 BHK apartment from his tax-free agricultural income from his 20 acres of land in remote Satara district which incidentally and 'unofficially' was barren land.

Interestingly, their only son Vijay was doing his M.S. in the USA after completing his Electrical Engineering from a Private Engineering College in Satara. It was rumoured that Vijay's G.R.E score was just 990 and that Mr. Aasholkar was spending over USD 200,000 on his M.S.

Joyce never liked the man. She thought that his gaze was lewd. In fact, he'd try to touch her in a 'friendly' way at every possible excuse. She remembered the incident when she was caught alone with him in the elevator.

"Serves him right!" She muttered with a shudder.

Her thoughts moved to Subbu... Apart from a good income and an apartment in a posh locality, she had nothing to show.

Subbu would work late every night and go to work unerringly on time. Even on weekends, he would get work home and be immersed in it.

She was alone, lonely, and longed to have a child. Unfortunately, Subbu was no help in that regard either. She was never in love with Subbu, but now she blamed him squarely for her boring existence.

The doorbell brought Joyce back to reality. It was Asha, the Aasholkar family maid, grinning from ear to ear as usual. "Wonder what she feels so happy about all the time?" thought Joyce and collected the magazine from her.

Even before she flipped open the magazine, an idea struck her...

Subbu had never tasted Soya Mince Cutlets, and both Mr. Aasholkar and Mr. Khosla would be too drunk to notice... what if...?

She chided herself for thinking the unthinkable. But the Chicken Cutlets refused to vacate her mind. In fact, it pervaded her mind.

"What the hell!" Joyce told herself, "I am entitled to at least some pleasures in life and it will teach the Iyers a lesson that they will never know they learnt."

Suddenly, the thought of Subbu eating chicken cutlets seemed extremely funny to her.

She imagined Iyer Senior screaming in his raspy voice "Subramanian... you have brought disrepute to the entire Iyer clan!"

But then, she knew that she had to take care that the truth was never out.

It was revenge... but only for herself. With a song on her lips, Joyce got dressed to visit the neighbourhood cold storage.

On the way, she bellowed ominously in her mind and muttered "Mugambo Khush Hua!". After all, not all villains were bald, ugly, murderous, and planned to take over the world!

~~~ THE BEGINNING OF THE END ~~~
~~~

2
REFLECTIONS

by Kavya Mithran

Why are people afraid of darkness? Its beauty, the silence in the night shadows, they are enchanting. The secrets these nights hold are my favourite. The murmuring of the trees...' Just then a peal of thunder roared outside. Jason woke up from his bizarre reflections.

'Ooh, this rain! You have distracted my musings again. Good thing that I closed the windows. I don't think this rain and thunder will let me sleep tonight. God, I am freezing. It was such a stupid idea not to bring a blanket with me.

And this bed is too small for me, very congested.'

He was restless and tried to be comfy, but he was cramped up. Jason was all alone there in pitch darkness.

'Will it be raining at home now? I hope Karthik is asleep. My little boy, he likes to play in the rain, but he gets terrified by the thunder. He even caught a fever once just because he splashed with you.'

Thunder rumbled again, but this time it was feeble. 'Was that an apology from the rain, for making my son sick?'

Jason laughed. 'Yes, you surely owe me an apology, rain. But it's okay. He should not have gone out while you were pouring down at your maximum.'

He lay there staring at the ceiling. 'I really miss my boy and Priya, I miss home. If she were with me now, just her presence would have made this place comfortable for me. Two-three weeks ago, all I wanted was to be left alone, to be away from all the problems. And now that I got what I wanted; my mind keeps telling me I was mistaken...'

"Karthik... he would always pester me to buy him toys. He had so many of the same kind. Yet, he would be so restless until he got them. But within a week or two, he would lose interest. Just like him, I am now bored with this lonely life. My way to life is my way to home, and I was too late to realize this. All I want now is to be back home."

Thunder crashed again. 'Hey, it looks like even the rain and thunder are sharing their happiness for me going back home tomorrow. Yes, I am leaving and can't bear another single day here.'

'Should I open the windows? I enjoy watching the rain...' But then another thought struck him. 'Those people in the neighbourhood may also be there outside. I don't want to start a conversation with them now. They always whisper behind my back because I am a newbie here. I hate it. Every night I can hear them chattering, it is more unbearable than the sound of crickets.'

Being fond of the darkness, he had decided to be within it and didn't want any shred of light to come inside. So, he had kept the windows shut. 'All these realizations, they have come to me now.. only during these sleepless nights in darkness, something the light couldn't shed within me. All these lonely days mattered the most for me, I now know all that matters is, being with my family, nothing else.' It was like his life was getting reflected before his eyes on that ceiling.

'Priya had managed everything at home, she was the rock of our family. All she wanted was our life to be peaceful, to be happy. When I spent all the money on alcohol and gambles, she saved every rupee for us. Even when the drugs got a complete hold on me and turned me to a monster. I abused and hurt her so badly, still, she never left my side. I still remember her pleading to me. "Please, Jason, listen to me. You can change, you can become my old Jason, please hear me out. This is where your heart is at, our son, our family, our home. Hold onto that. I want you back. This monster is so not you, don't let him control."

'Oh God, I didn't even let her finish. The next thing I did was to slap her and scream at her. How could I?'

Jason couldn't control his tears. He wanted to cry out loud. He wanted to scream his apologies, but the words were stuck somewhere inside.

'What a demon I have been! Believing my wicked company of so-called "friends", I found beating and abusing her as a symbol of my masculinity and taking charge of my control over her. How pathetic. How cruel I have been! I was insecure and being hateful. But all for nothing. Her pain, all those scars I left. No sacred ritual can cleanse me of my actions.'

Though he found the cold freezing his bones, his heart was melting under the heat of his guilt. 'I was such a coward. I couldn't even face the consequences of my own actions. Even when in that enormous debt, Priya had always asked me to stay strong. She worked hard to rescue our family, a sinking ship. It was all because of me. And all I did was abandon my family, leave everything and escape. I left her and our son all alone. I left them and hid in this place far away from them. And here I am alone, away from all those problems, but with a heart aching twice as before.'

His tears flowed freely. The rain was getting stronger outside.

'It was a rainy day like today when I held my Karthik for the first time. How tiny he was! Priya was the happiest on that day. And all I had ever wanted was to be a good father which I never was. I could never be one. My little boy, he would now picture me as a monster. The one who caused his mom pain, the one who never gave him even a happy smile for the past two years, the father who always shouted, the one who never went to his PTA meetings. The father who was never there for him. Every father wants to be the hero in his son's life story, but I am the villain in my son's story. I am the villain in everyone's story, in Priya's, in Karthik's. No person will ever wish to become the villain in their son's story. But here I am, living the darkest dreams, nightmares, of any man.'

His body shook as he sobbed, unable to contain his grief anymore.

'I had thought the pleasures in life were all in drugs and partying every single day. How shallow I had been! Like a hypocrite, I had cursed the villains in movies, when they killed or harmed someone. But what I did was much worse, worse than any villain, worse than taking someone's life! I had sucked out the soul of happiness from my family. I ruined everything.'

Minutes passed, he was still immersed in his thoughts. The tears had stopped by now. With a deep breath, he decided, 'I must rewrite my story. I should go back and bring back the happiness in my family. Make our house a home again. Yes, I am going back tomorrow and no more mistakes. It has been almost a month since I left home. Will they let me in? Even if she beats me, scolds me, or curses me, I'd let her.. she is right as I am bound to get them all. Will Karthik accept me as his father? I don't know.'

The rain was much lighter outside. 'Let me get some sleep now. I will wake up early tomorrow and go home.'

He closed his eyes and tried to get some sleep.

Footsteps approached his room. There were two people.. Jason hastily opened his eyes and thought, 'I feel Karthik and Priya are somewhere near me!'

He glanced around him and then thought, ' No... How foolish I am! They would never know this place. I am imagining things. Maybe because of the excitement of going home. Let me sleep.'

Outside, Priya and Karthik stood. Priya held an umbrella in one hand and Karthik's little finger in another. Karthik had a bouquet in his tiny hand. Priya's sunken tear-stained eyes revealed her heart whimpering in pain. As she neared him, more tears came running down.

'Amma, why are you crying? Don't cry Amma, we are here to see Pappa. If you cry he also will be sad. Please don't cry, Amma', Karthik's voice called out to her.

'I am not crying, child. It's okay. Come, let's go closer to Pappa.'

They walked along the cemetery and reached a corner. Karthik stood on his knees and placed the bouquet on a plaque.

3

COLOUR OF MUD

by Ar. Jerin Jo Thomas

December, AD 2031

Alyne strolled along, admiring the surrounding crowd. She walked past many artists and art stalls as if she was walking around a flea market in a nomad camp. People of different cultures and languages walked past her. She couldn't help but notice how happy everyone looked. A girl with a blue butterfly face painting below her left eye stopped by Alyne, chatted for a while, showing off her sublime card skills and laughing out loud. Every wall around her, drenched in brilliant colours and graffiti, stood tall telling a thousand stories. The old buildings of the market were transformed into art shops, cafes, and studios. An Asian chef was carefully hand-pulling noodles behind a glass wall. As she walked along the central vista, she found a large wooden signboard saying, "YOU HAVE SUCCESSFULLY FOUND THE HEART OF THE NOMAD GROUP." She knew in her heart - this rustic blue door on that ivy-covered stone wall was where she was going to find answers for everything she wanted to know.

Cafe OBASI was calm as always, as Alyne slowly crossed the peepal, and found the perfect spot under the canopy of the catclaw, with its impressive blend of yellow and green. She sat beside the Buddha statue, and just like everyone else, she was awestruck by the elegance and serenity of that place. The chirping of birds, the humming of bees, rustling of leaves and the gurgle of the small waterfall filled the space with a divine charm. She looked around and embraced this perfect example of adaptive reuse. The old buildings of Changanacherry market were converted into perfect spots to portray tropical modernism. Somebody had worked their magic there, and she was there to know more about that mastermind. Siva approached Alyne with his ever-charming smile to take her order and her words were clearly premeditated, "I'd like to have a doppio, and a talk about JJ."

***

The evening sun had already passed Changanacherry on its journey towards the Arabian sea beyond the coast of Alappuzha, as Sunnychan walked in quick strides along the steps of the boat jetty towards the Anchuvilakku. With a smouldering beedi between his lips and a small black pouch and the free end of his lungi being held in his left armpit, he moved past some couples enjoying the beautiful evening. He strode past Megha and Maathan rehearsing for the big eve tomorrow, with Maathan strumming the guitar and his flute waiting right next to him for its turn, a few kids from the market trying their luck to catch one more fish before it gets too dark, and their Amma yelling at them from a distance, Chandran and few other porters having another intense round of rummy, and as always, Niyati reading a book, with Bacardi sleeping peacefully right next to her legs.

***

Cafe OBASI had already been a conjunction point for artists from all around the globe, and these old streets of the market and the decades-old buildings had their fate redefined just by that man. This community of artists, this place where people live with no limits to their imagination and happiness, this hell of an everyday carnival, it definitely feels like a Utopia of its own kind, all thanks to that visionary. When JJ brought his design studio to this old marketplace, nobody knew what he was about to do. Nobody, even his close ones, thought his ideas would be possible to the scale in which it is now. The small design studio and cafe they started, now had its root deep down into the very soul of Changanacherry, and its branches reaching everywhere where art has a say, and only the man himself knew how he managed to visualize this change.

***

Rajan was on his knees, bent over, his forehead touching the plastic sheet spread on the floor. He was crying like a kid who lost his favourite toy. He was all alone in that construction site; the gates were neither shut, nor he was tied up. Yet, he couldn't run. He was frozen like a cold winter night in the Alps. He knew he fucked up from the moment he realized the man he tried to mess up with was actually the Devil himself.

***

Sunnychan reached his tea-stall and had another look at the Dali face graffiti drawn on the vertical folding wooden shutters by some kids for the carnival. He opened them, and the kettle went right on. He was disturbed and anxious, anyone could easily decipher that from his face. He took the phone out from his pocket and dialled.

***

Siva approached Alyne and gave her a small note. She looked confused as she hurried out of OBASI and turned towards the anchuvilakku.

"What do you want, lady? Who are you?"

She looked around and found Sunnychan sitting on a small bench in his tea-stall, enjoying a beedi.

"You asked for me."

Alyne took three steps towards the tea-stall, had a look around. This guy with grey hair and moustache was alone there, and oddly enough, nobody else came to that stall even though it was the peak hour.

"You wanted to talk about JJ, and who knows in which hell he is now. So, I'm the best option you got."

"I know JJ is more than whatever he seems to the outside world. I mean no trouble, but I want the truth. I want to talk to him if possible."

Suddenly, Sunnychan started laughing, puzzling her.

"See for yourself, kid. Look around you! Everything you see and everything hidden in this market.. all of this is JJ. The fate of this place turned upside down because of him, and I don't think you need any better explanation."

***

That matte black Dodge Challenger appeared again on the streets of Changanacherry, out of nowhere, and it took everyone by surprise. The most famous car in the town it was, but few knew that its boss was back. It gathered momentum as it turned left from the Central Junction towards Kottayam and glided past a thousand surprised eyes. Those bronze alloy wheels made it look as if it was hovering just above the road. Tyres squeaked as it left MC Road and went inside the mud building under construction on the right side of the road beyond Palathrachira.

***

The sky was slowly turning red and the market was already flooded with people. Artists were all set to showcase their skills to the public in their shops and stalls. Every nook and cranny was decorated and reflected happiness. Food stalls were running in full swing, crafting the flavours from around the globe, and the air was filled with the complex aroma from countless spices.

Leaning onto the handrails near the anchuvilakku, Alyne lit a cigarette, gazing into the red horizon. Niyati was there on her usual spot, a few meters away from Alyne, and Bacardi guarding her as always, and as peaceful as it can be. "Lazy dog", Alyne told herself as she blew out another cloud of smoke. Salimkka was busy making sarbath from his homemade Goli Soda and some announcements started blaring off the loudspeakers. The area was tightly packed, and suddenly out of nowhere, Bacardi jumped up as if she smelled something familiar. She jumped around Niyati in excitement, and started barking, with her eyes fixed on a small boat approaching the docks. Niyati was surprised and the entire regular faces of the market were puzzled, seeing Bacardi unusually excited. As she trotted towards the boat, Niyati closed the book and stood up, and Alyne put the cigarette down and crushed it with the tip of her boot.

A dark figure jumped onto the deck, with a carelessly done topknot of his hair, a few strands falling over his face, and long curly beard. Bacardi stood there, right in front of him, took another look and sniff, and all of a sudden, she started jumping all around him in excitement. Alyne was amazed, and she was eager to know who that is. He looked like a nomad himself, wearing a dark long-sleeved half kurta and joggers, carrying a backpack and sling bag, and those eyes, even from the distance Alyne could tell, were as unfathomable as the ocean.

He started walking towards the anchuvilakku, with Bacardi trailing behind him. The closer he came, the more Alyne's tongue dried up. Some voice inside her head whispered, "JJ.."

He walked towards Niyati, and she too was overjoyed, just like Bacardi. They hugged, and he lifted her up. She burst into tears of joy, and they both started laughing. Bacardi was still running around them. Maathan and Megha were on the stage, about to start their session when Megha noticed some guy hugging Niyati and Bacardi energetic as she was in old times. Maathan followed her gaze, and in no time, they both knew who it was. Maathan screamed into the mike loud, "JJ..!!!" and, done, the market went dead silent for a moment before breaking into one hell of an applause. He started walking towards the stage slowly, to witness another version of this celebration that he started right there years before. Stalls stopped sales, street artists stopped their performances, and people started flowing into the already flooded arena.

Even though she knew the influence this man had in this town, Alyne never expected it to be this humongous. He got onto the stage, hugged Maathan and Megha, and looked around. Loose strands of his hair were dancing in the gentle evening wind, and he made a perfect silhouette against the red evening sky. Accompanied with that ever-slow gaze of those deep eyes, he lifted his left fist, covered in a black glove, towards the sky, and with its rise, the crowd went silent again, just like old times.

***

"So, you wanted to know more about me. Here I am."

JJ walked in with two cups of tea and handed one over to Alyne. She was shocked by this unexpected confrontation and threw her cigarette down. JJ crushed it under his feet, picked it up and dumped it in a trash can nearby.

"This is how we stay like whatever we are."

"I'm sorry I wasn't myself.. I..."

"Look around you. This market, and my business revolving around and beyond these streets... This is who I am."

"But there are so many dots still not connected.."

"Be my guest. See for yourself and you'll understand. If you'll excuse me now, I've to deal with some important business matters. See ya tomorrow!"

***

Tyres squeaked as the Challenger stopped outside the construction site, and Rajan grew pale with fear. He didn't have the strength to turn around and look back. Pigeons were feasting on the rice husk used to create building blocks, they were the only witnesses to his helplessness. JJ emerged from the car, clad in his Devil attire. That perfect black suit, and the perfect topknot and neatly combed beard. Everything was black from the necktie to the shoes, and he held his favourite weapon in his left hand. That katana exhibited at OBASI was actually being put to use at times, unknown to the public. They didn't know he was a gifted swordsman. Rajan choked on his own words, and moreover, the time for words had already been over. JJ unsheathed the katana slowly and placed the blade, near the hilt, on Rajan's throat, looked him in the eyes, and Rajan realized the ever-present calmness in those eyes was actually a perfect veil for the eyes of the Devil. JJ smiled at Rajan and glided the sword effortlessly. His eyes rolled, and Rajan fell to his right side with a thud, his hands about to reach his throat. He lay there, in a pool of blood on the plastic wrap, as JJ cleaned the blade on his blue denim jeans. The katana went back inside the sheath as JJ walked towards the Challenger, and a thousand pigeons took off from the ground making a loud noise.

***

Huge trucks carrying ready-mix earthcrete and mud mixtures for rammed earth became a regular sight around Changanacherry as JJ implemented more sustainable buildings there, and in one of those trucks, the ground remnants of Rajan were getting mixed up with the mud mixture to make the bright shades on some rammed-earth walls.

***

The Challenger stopped in front of the construction site again. JJ and Alyne came out and he was in his black attire again.

"This is the building I've been telling you about. It'll be the next big thing in Kerala Architecture, this five-storeyed corporate office created with hemp blocks, shall be the first of its kind in Kerala."

He guided her into the empty building.

"You didn't tell me about this black version of yours.."

"It's nothing. I've always loved black. I wear them for some special dates."

Alyne smiled as she walked into the building, admiring the unique texture on the rammed earth show walls. The shades and patterns were clearly out of the world.

"The colour of mud." She whispered to herself.

Even though she knew this guy's brain worked in alien ways, she was awestruck by that building.

"Hi there Halime!"

Alyne grew pale in the fraction of a second. She couldn't believe what she just heard and turned around slowly. JJ was there, looking deep into her eyes and the katana in his right hand, unsheathed.

"So, you thought it'd be easy to come into my empire, trick my people, kill me and just leave like that? I know everything about you Alyne, I mean Halime Nasser, everything, including that poisoned dagger you always carried inside your boots." She hurried to check her boots. "Relax. That's safe with Siva."

Halime started sweating like never before. She knew it was time and went down on her knees. She saw hell in those deep eyes as the blade glided slowly over her neck.

Trucks carrying mud mixtures diverged into various locations from Changanacherry that day as well.

4

BUT IT'S DESTINY

by Aaqilah A J

Darla realized that she had once again zoned out into her own fantasy in the middle of her Math class. But she was a bit late in shaking it off, for Ms. Ak47 had already noticed Darla's inattentiveness.

"Okay. So now, who can tell me about the range of Cos functions?" shot Ms. Ak47.

"Please don't ask me. Please don't ask me," whispered Darla as if it was gonna save her. After all, Ms. Doris had particularly asked this question so that she could call out Darla. Amidst all that hands going up, Ms. Doris pointed out, "Yes Darla. I would love to hear it from you."

"Ahh... emm... The range... Can you please repeat the question, ma'am?" stuttered Darla, making it easier for Ms. Ak47 to aim.

"Oh! That's fabulous. Our Darla had once again turned on her stargazer mode. Kindly don't disturb her, everybody. She is busy zoning out." Giving a little interval for the class to laugh at Darla, Ms. Doris shouted, "OUT! NOW!" Darla was left with no choice but to go out - and have some fun. Ha! She had to stand there, staring into nothing, which was her hobby anyway.

"Anybody else?" asked Ms. Dorris.

One hand went up. It was none other than Mr. Know-It-All. "Between -1 and 1," said Martin casually, but proudly enough to offend Darla. But this wasn't anything new. It was pretty regular for Darla to zone out and be punished for that.

The sound of the bell came as a relief to all those students who were on the verge of falling asleep. Ms. Dorris, however, wouldn't dismiss the class until one last problem was solved.

***

"Why do you always get caught in her class? If you're going to daydream, at least be sneaky about it. Must you always make it obvious? I am ashamed of you, my friend. All those years of teaching have gone in vain," chastised Emily as soon as she saw Darla after class.

"Oh, my guru, I am so sorry to have disappointed you. I was trying my best. But you know, Ms. Ak47 has really sharp eyes. And I've been shot by her for quite a few times now for it to matter anymore," explained Darla, cleverly masking her sarcasm with a straight face.

They shared a laugh as they packed their things. The school was over, but it was Darla and Emily's turn to clean the classroom. So, they waited until everybody else left the class.

"Why is the class the messiest just when it is our turn to clean?" muttered Darla as she started picking up all the litter. "My dearest friend, Darla, I love you so much. You're the best friend I could have asked for. It must not be a big deal to do it all by yourself," said Emily, as she made an innocent face.

"No! No way! I am not letting you go today. You owe me, anyway. So, why don't you do it all by yourself?" Darla demanded.

"Hey! I got you! I was just kidding. I would never ask you to do it alone. We'll do it together. Okay?" managed Emily, as she blew a flying kiss to Darla.

The banter made their job easier. They finished cleaning the classroom in no time. As they were about to leave the class, Emily said, "Darla, look. There is a book under that table. Someone must have left it behind."

***

Darla was about to turn back and head to the bus stop when she saw someone going towards the construction site. The school was building a new hall for no particular reason. They just thought building a new hall near the library will be beneficial somehow. But the work had stopped a few days back.

The person was wearing the same uniform that she wore. After looking more keenly, she thought she figured out who it was.

It was 4:30 already, but it was as if the sun didn't want to set. But, suddenly, as though the clouds couldn't bear the bright radiance emitted by the seemingly happy sun, it started to drizzle. Darla ran to find some shelter under the trees nearby. She stood there, waiting for the sun to show up again. But the clouds didn't want to give up either. She looked at her watch and realized that it was almost five. If she wasn't home by 5:30, her impossibly vicious Aunt May might as well put her under house arrest. Yes! Darla was the Cinderella of her household except that she had a really mean aunt instead of a step-mother. No one really cared if she was alive or dead, except for those few friends in school.

Darla's aunt was least bothered by the fact that Darla could be stuck somewhere. In fact, she continued cursing Darla, "That ill-mannered wench! Doesn't she know to come home after school? It's 6'o o'clock already."

"Will you give it a rest, May? Why do you even care?" said Uncle Rex, who was in no way better than Aunt May.

"Is that mannerless girl staying over at Emily's again without informing me? Let me call her and teach her a lesson." Aunt May whipped out her phone when suddenly it started ringing.

"Oh, Hello Mrs. Park! Oh, damn! I forgot. I will be there in fifteen minutes." Aunt May hung up.

"I am going shopping with Mrs. Park. Do not call me unless it is really important," Aunt May informed Uncle Rex before leaving. Darla's aunt did not realize that Darla had not reached home until a day after. She tried calling her, not because she was worried, but because she was furious. Darla's phone was switched off. Aunt May called Emily to ask if she was aware of Darla's whereabouts. But Emily was clueless as well. Finally, after realizing that no one knew where Darla was, Aunt May and Uncle Rex decided to inform the police.

The police enquired all the students in the school. They found Darla's mobile in her school locker. Emily was the last person to meet Darla. She started recounting that day's events to the police.

***

"Ah! It seems like Mr. Know-It-All left his math book behind. What is he going to do about it? I don't think he will be able to sleep tonight. Poor Martin!" Emily had said as she made a face.

"I'll return it to him." Darla had quipped, her eyes lighting up with excitement.

"Now look who is jumping at an opportunity to meet him. You cunning Darla! But I doubt Martin even recognizes your existence," Emily had said, letting out a sigh.

"No, Ely," Darla tried to hide her smile, "I am just trying to help. You know, it's a good habit." She had grinned.

"Oh Darla, I didn't know that you were this kind-hearted," Emily had smiled. "Anyways, I'll head home first. My parents wanted me to accompany them to Mr. Harry's home. Bye then!"

"Okay, bye then," Darla had waved as she saw Emily walk down the road.

***

But Martin told the police that he hadn't met Darla at all. He stood firm in his statement. Having neither any surveillance footage nor any lead in the case, the police soon had to close the case unsolved. Darla's aunt and uncle couldn't care less to take the case to higher officials.

Like that, Darla slowly started vanishing from everyone's memory; except Emily's, of course. Emily didn't want to give up on her friend. She wanted to know what had happened to her best friend. But what could a helpless teenage girl do, when even the police were unable to proceed with the investigation?

The days passed as usual. The one thing that seemed off was that Martin was no longer Mr. Know-It-All. He grew more and more aggressive. Everyone soon knew that something was wrong with him.

Months passed like days, and the day that all students were looking forward to, or rather dreading, finally arrived. It was the day of the final exams. The school had suddenly decided to finish the construction and it was in a hall in that building that the students were going to take their final exams.

A feeling of terror stuck Martin as he walked down the cold corridors on the day of the exam. It just worsened the condition of his already weak self.

****

Darla followed the person to the construction site, as she wondered what business he had in an unfinished construction site. "He wouldn't go there without any reason. Maybe something came up. Anyways, it's good that I saw him here," she convinced herself.

It was then when it started to drizzle. She stood under a tree waiting for the clouds to give up. But eventually, she was the one who had to give up. She ran quickly into the construction site. As she entered the construction site, a weird feeling of fear took over her.

***

"Everyone, do well in your exam. First of all, everyone check if you are seated at the right table," The invigilator continued with the other instructions.

Fate seemed to be at play, because Martin sat right above the place where poor Darla was buried. Ignorant of that fact, Martin started writing the exam. But an inner tingling feeling warned him that something was definitely wrong.

A few minutes passed by.

Everything seemed to go perfectly until Martin suddenly noted blood in his paper. Was he hallucinating? He wasn't. The blood was dripping from his nose. Before he could process what was happening, he started coughing blood. He rested his head on the table and suddenly, he realized that he was going to die.

The memories of that day came flooding to him.

As soon as Darla entered the building, she was relieved that it was the person whom she assumed it was. She saw Martin, sitting in the other corner of the building facing the wall. He was holding something which Darla assumed was a book. She called out, "Martin, you left your -" She couldn't finish her sentence as she figured out that Martin was not holding books in his hands. 'The handsome, smart and charming Martin is taking drugs' was all that she could think of.

Before her reflexes told her that she was in the wrong place at the wrong time, witnessing something she shouldn't have, he grabbed her by the arm. "What are you doing here?" he barked.

"I was just -" Darla couldn't find her words. "I came to return your math textbook, " she finished, trembling so hard that she almost collapsed.

"Oh! Okay," Martin sighed, relaxing visibly before speaking further, "Listen, it's not what you think it is. I can explain. These are - " But Darla was not ready to hear any further. She wanted to leave. The only thing her head told her was to get out of there. She tried to loosen his hold which was of no use. The various techniques she used to escape only made the situation worse. Finally, she gathered all her strength and stamped him on his feet and pushed him away. A furious Martin tried to stop her. In his quick attempt, he tried to grab her hair which caused Darla to lose her balance.

Darla fell hard and hurt her leg. She couldn't move. Her white socks were soaked with blood. As Darla sat there, crying and pleading Martin to let her go, Martin sighed and slowly sat beside her. He started, "Darla, I know you must think that I am a freak and that I am a drug addict. But - " But Darla wouldn't listen to a single word he said. She kept sobbing and repeating the same words, "Let me go. Let me go."

Martin lost his patience. "Will you shut up?" he shouted and hit her on the head with a stone that lay nearby. It was as though a monster buried inside Martin had woken up. Darla lay there, unconscious. Martin just sat there, smiling like a psycho.

Then slowly, he got hold of his syringe. He filled a full dosage of the drug in the syringe and stabbed it right into her radial vein. He sat there smiling at her, until she eventually stopped breathing.

The hero she had a crush on becoming the villain of her own life was the last thing Darla could have ever dreamt of. Just like that, poor Darla's heart gave up on her.

Now that she was dead, Martin had to deal with the corpse. He quickly thought of a way to get rid of it. He found a crowbar nearby and started to dig. He slowly dragged Darla's corpse and put her into the pit he dug. Then, using the same crowbar, he closed the pit and made sure that it looked like how it was.

It was not until the next morning that Martin's inner monster was put to sleep again. As soon as Martin realized what he had done, guilt overwhelmed him. But a part of him kept telling him that it wasn't his fault, that it was just the circumstances.

And it was this part of him that made him act all innocent, pretending that nothing happened.

Amidst all these thoughts flashing before Martin's eyes, "Darla", he gasped as he closed his eyes, never to open them up again. It was probably his guilt that was eating him from the inside.

All the students gathered around Martin. Medical help was called. Everyone was looking at Martin, except for Emily. She was looking at something else, the blood-covered paper on Martin's table.

Tears filled her eyes as she read Martin's last words.

"What if I was born first to my parents? What if they loved me as much as they loved my brother? What if I hadn't developed bipolar? What if I didn't have to keep it a secret from everyone else? What if I didn't go to the construction site that day? What if Darla never saw me taking my medicines? What if she was patient enough to listen? What if I hadn't become a monster that day?" Martin had wondered.

Even if any one of those situations had not happened, Darla would still be alive. And he wouldn't have lived dying with guilt every moment. But, it must have been his destiny. Darla's too.

We do things, not having the slightest hint that we will be regretting it for the rest of our lives. And just like that, we unintentionally become the villain of someone's life. And the worst-case is when that someone turns out to be none other than us.

5

INSIDE THE BEAUTIFUL MIND OF A LUNATIC

by Shrey Sharma

The night is still young and the crowd is drowning in the blinding city lights with the sound of Rock and Blues. The era of classics as they would say, The Mesmerizing 70's. When life was supposed to be a little off the edge or was it always the glimmering limelight of shining gold chains and cigarette butts.

I wonder how bad it would be to live knowing there is no peace and an eye always lurking in the corner to take you out. The adrenaline to live on the tip of your toes, running not away from the enemy but to execute a massacre!

The beautiful mind of a criminal, as I would love to frame it, was always an intriguing picture to paint in my mind, yet I wondered how far I've come to be so immersed in the matter! The sirens going off, yet subtle as the wind he executed his masterpiece to perfection with only one question to ask the city of Miami.

"Was it enough?"

I studied 'Him' for a long time yet there was this feeling of curiosity as if I was missing a part of the puzzle. There was a certain set of emotion that was missing while I tried to picture 'Him' because there was no story about him! No phrase, no explanation, or an origin to look into, yet 'He' felt so complete as if Miami was his mistress and he, the undisputed king!

Eventually, there will be a time when we all keep digging the graves that were never meant to be touched and we end up unravelling the truth that was savoured as the sacred hymn for humanity! It was something similar that rattled once a magnificent man who cherished life beyond measures and hailed Miami as his beloved! 'He' was the kingpin of the city and was loved by all.

However not every king can reign for eternity and sooner or later there shall be a rebellion needed to be settled. The thirst for power drives one insane and the greed to command and love the city you grew up in was more of a hit on the ego of his prodigy, when he decided to leave for good and end the legacy 'He' created the kid was not okay letting the empire fall.

James was like his own boy and 'He' loved him with all his life, 'He' adored James for all the reasons a father would adore his son. In spite of the fact that James was one of the boys he picked from the streets and gave him a life apart from the drugs and sex in the city, James was hungry for more! He wanted it all, the name, the game, the rep and the fame that came with his legacy.

As the sun drowned into the horizon turning the daylight to dusk, there was a sinister eeriness that evening. A diabolic plan was to be executed as James was drenched in the high of power, he wanted to end this all and claim the 'Hardy empire!' As 'His' sleep sounded like an angel's lullaby, the bare footsteps of the devil whispered in the wind, the boy he loved so dearly was standing tall above him. 'He' always told James that the most beautiful way to kill someone is not to pull the trigger and shoot them dead but to systematically take away everything that person holds close to his heart and slit their throat with a Surgical Knife as it was 'His' favourite, Watch the person live the agony of losing everything he loved along with witnessing the betrayal that he would have never imagined!

James thought of all the moments he had with 'Him' and before anyone knew he slit his throat and there was a deafening silence, with a stream of crimson on the sheets James finally claimed the throne of the Hardy empire! He showed off 'His' lifeless body to instil fear and asked the men to dispose of his body to feed to wild animals. Was that really the end of the one king that ruled Miami? The King of the Hardy empire?

Months passed and James was now used to being the king of Miami, all the drug cartels, the mansion, the name, the reputation came along with the Hardy name! He was the king of the world! But what he was not aware of this that he was not the only person who was taught to be ready for the worst.

'He' was a mastermind who ruled the city of Miami for more than a decade and he knew he would be carrying a target on his back all the time, so he began the plot to find out what was going on when he noticed that James was acting strange. He kept a close look and observed and eventually he was able to figure out while having a conversation with James that he had his eyes on the empire.

'He' knew he was in danger.

On the night when James was going to execute his plan, 'He' was prepared to execute a plot of his own. Before he went in his room to sleep he went to get himself fixed, he called in a surgeon who stitched another layer of skin around his neck which had a diamond-coated sheet within to stop the blade reaching his neck so that he doesn't end up getting killed. When James swung the knife thinking he killed the man, he actually didn't but went on to cement 'His' plan.

'He' then went underground to prepare for vengeance, one not for the city he loved but for the betrayal he has received by the hands of the boy he loved so dearly. Day in and day out he disguised himself as a commoner to see how things were now taking place in Miami, the police were pushing towards the Hardy empire and James was busy enjoying the luxury. It's truly said, "There is nothing that can make you more vulnerable than the desire to have what you wish to have the most!"

And James was the perfect example of it at the moment.

Meanwhile, 'He' on the other hand was prepared to lay waste on the empire and the city he built which was snatched away from him. What was it that pushed him so much that he was about to decimate the city he loved was to be answered, truly the rage within was a factor to add yet what drove him the most was the one thing he didn't expect or calculate when his execution by the hands of James took place. His love, the woman only James was aware about was alone as well and after James was done executing him, he straight went for Penelope. She was the girl that no one knew, a part of his world only James knew and the part which he decided to destroy.

After 'He' was disposed of by the men he went to check her only to find Penelope's house all shattered and broken. He walked through the broken glass on the floor with stains of blood, He could sense there was something wrong and someone had forced their way into the house and as soon as he reached the room he found her corpse naked bathed in blood. There were cuts on her entire body with a smile carved on her face and breast chopped off, she was raped and killed by the person He loved the most. James was a dead man walking now!

While 'He' was grounded planning to avenge the death of Penelope and the betrayal he got, James decided to throw a masquerade ball for the night of New Year's Eve! That was the window 'He' was looking for, when finally, bodies shall be engraved in ice and when the blood within the vein freezes! When the smirk of Satan will be His as He would devour souls to burn into ashes, cemetery gates awaiting to be unlocked with the reaper holding invitation with dripping crimson from the blade's sharp edge!

It was the night of the masquerade, the entire city was invited and James being an adrenaline junkie had all the guests to play a game of Russian Roulette! The only catch was the guns were fake and would leave smoke when triggered with ammunition.

A picture-perfect opportunity to create chaos for 'Him' yet he preferred the subtle art of dismantling the senses of James one by one! As soon as the roulette began, 'HE' switched one the guns with a real Magnum revolver for the fourth couple to try and as it was James' idea, his best friend Dino and his girlfriend Amanda were to play the 4th round. Oh, the fun was about to begin as Amanda fired her brains out on the floor and there was havoc all over the place. The best part that happened was when 'He' entered the facility. He locked all the doors and swapped the keys with the guards.

James knew he was doomed as someone had risen to make sure he falls! Lurking into the shadows hidden behind the mask began the dance of death as 'He' went on to kill every ally James relied on and as he did there were messages written in blood all over the floor!

"Run!" It said and fear instilled within the heart of James he knew he was on the verge of losing it all. James ran upstairs to his armoury to get his pistol and to his surprise, the inventory was empty, a message written in blood!

"Did you forget, I told you to keep your friends close but your weapons even closer!" A rattling sound of a pistol thrown on the floor, James knew who was present there!

"I wouldn't expect this, but it seems you have outworked me again, Uncle Ming!" James said.

"I feel sorry James, you didn't make sure I was dead. If you were to take away all I had, my breath should have been the first thing you should have checked!" Ming said.

Lightning struck and with it fell the body of Dino, with blood pumping out of his neck and leaving James frozen as if he had seen a ghost.

'He' stood in front of him, with the same surgical knife he loved the most! Trembling with fear of death knocking his doors James knelt before him to beg for mercy and Ming looked into his eyes with the blade around his neck and said:

"You would have had it all as the heir to the Hardy Empire, but you chose to snatch it away. I would have given it up happily, but you made the one mistake I warned you about, taking away the humanity within me and turning me into a cold-blooded demon that has no remorse!"

Slitting his throat 'He' claimed his vengeance and hung the naked body of James outside the city centre with a message for the world

"In order to win a war, make sure the enemy has something to lose because there is nothing more dangerous than a man who has nothing to lose!"

With a sinister smile and tears down his cheeks, Ming Hardy claimed the city he loved and killed the child he loved the most! He was no longer the King of Miami, but he was the name of a reigning terror that knew no emotions, a man turned into a cold-blooded animal with no feelings or emotions to die for!

And that was the story of the legend that ruled Miami, the psychology of a serial killer who once was a human! A person who loved someone beyond his own capacity and heart, who gave his soul to a child and got his heart ripped out!

Ming Hardy is the name that everyone fears and till date, there is a part of me that hopes it wouldn't have happened!

After all, "I lost my innocence when James decided to take it all!"

I don't know if I'll remember it all because 'He' might return to erase it all!

Hahahaha!!!

Date: July 13' 1974
Entry: Ming "Ryan" Hardy

6

THE ABSENT KING OF GANDHARA

by Amritha Suryakumar

The rays of the afternoon sun, escaping through the foliage of the Neem tree, cast its warmth on me. I was taking a stroll in the garden in anticipation of the arrival of the Pandavas.

"Are you going to deceive the Pandavas into gambling everything they hold dear to them, dear Father Shakuni?" I heard a troubled voice call out to me.

Startled, I turned around to find my son, Uluka, the handsome-crown prince of Gandhara, his brows arched in worry. He grew up in the neglect of his father and the absence of his mother. I could see his mother, queen Arshi in his soft eyes and pensive nose. "It's a friendly game between the cousins, the Pandavas and the Kauravas. It's not uncommon for kings to invite his allies for such a game, occasionally, Uluka", I quickly assured him. I knew, he questioned me, because my name, "Shakuni" was already synonymous with deceit in Hastinapura. However, Uluka refused to believe it.

I knew my answer had not completely convinced him; his distrusting eyes followed the subtle limp in my walk. How he found it in him to love me, despite my negligence of him, I would never know. If only, I could tell him, how revenge gnawed at my being, how my quivering mind knew no rest. But it was too dangerous to bear one's heart, even if it was with one's son. I would never let anyone walk into the trenches of my heart. A part of me wanted to protect him from the destruction that was to ensue, the destruction that I would be the catalyst for. He was, after all, my precious son. I tried in vain to send him to Gandhara to his mother and his maternal uncle, who oversaw the administration of Gandhara. But he had taken a vow to never leave Hastinapura until I did, and it was against Kshatriya dharma to break one's vows. So, he stayed with me, willing to brave through the raging storm that would engulf the kingdom of Hastinapura. As if he could read my thoughts, he said, "Father, I have a premonition that the game will lead to adverse consequences!"

"A true prince never shies away from challenges, Dear Uluka. I promise to protect myself and you", I said, looking away from his eyes. We headed back to the palace for an early supper. All through the night, I could hear the agitated footsteps of Uluka across the long corridors, outside my chambers. For the first time, I could feel guilt tugging at my heart, but I could not let these emotions stand in my way. I reminded myself of my life's purpose and resisted the urge to let Uluka into the secret that was tormenting me.

Morning came, bringing with it, the Pandavas and their wife, Draupadi. Duryodhana and I were on the grand staircase leading to the palace, to receive the entire party. Almost immediately, I noticed the contemptuous smile on Duryodhana's face. He had awaited this day, as much as I had. Little did he know, he was a mere pawn in my carefully orchestrated play!

"Today, I will defeat those proud Pandavas and make them beg me for mercy, Mama Shakuni. Yudhishthira is no match to your prowess in the game of dice", scorned Duryodhana. I knew that the Maya Sabha of the Pandavas in Indraprastha had rekindled his jealousy and he longed to make it his own. He had turned to me to help him like he always did. But I ached for something else, something that even the cunning Duryodhana was not capable of imagining. "But how do we ensure Yudhisthira continues the game for as long as we want him to?" Duryodhana continued. He seemed almost fixated on defeating the Pandavas by any means. I whispered, "Yudhishthira may be the most virtuous in the entire kingdom of Hastinapura, but he secretly nurses an addiction for the game of dice. With a little prodding, I will be able to engage him in the game for as long as I want".

I noticed Sahadeva, the youngest of the brothers, walking towards me. Smiling warily at me, he said, "I hope we will see you in the Sabha for the game of dice, Mama". He bowed to touch my feet and walked away. Sahadeva was the calmest, most knowledgeable of the brothers. The Pandavas were virtuous enough to treat me with respect, despite their animosity with Duryodhana.

The assertive gait and poised demeanour of Draupadi caught my attention. It reminded me of my unfortunate sister, Gandhari in her younger days, before she was married off to the blind king, Dhritarashtra. I will never forget how she was terrified of darkness as a young girl and every evening was spent in lighting the numerous lamps that filled her apartment quarters. But after her marriage, she took it as her dharma, as a wife, to not enjoy the sights of the world, which her husband could not. The bards sing poetic praises, glorifying her blindfolding herself as the ultimate sacrifice and love for her husband. But I have never approved of Dhritarashtra. His lack of sight did not affect me as much as his lack of vision as a ruler did. He was no match to my beautiful, brave and ambitious sister. This is one of the many reasons why, I never will forgive Dhritarashtra and Bhishma, the guardian of the Kuru Dynasty. He had arrived at our royal court in Gandhara, with an entourage of well-armed warriors. Being a small kingdom, we knew we could never turn the proposal down without facing the Might and the wrath of the powerful, Kuru army. Unhappily, Gandhari had accepted the proposal to save our family and the kingdom of Gandhar.

Meanwhile, the Sabha was ready for the Game of dice. Duryodhana had taken a special interest in the construction of the Sabha, to flaunt his wealth to the Pandavas. His entire life was about proving to the Pandavas that he was their equal, if not better. The royal architects and engineers had invested their sweat and blood to build this grand Sabha. The finest of silks and fabric beautifully adorned the podium at the centre of the Sabha. Soon, the most prominent members of the royal court of Hastinapura took their seats. I could also see the king of Anga, Karna in the Sabha. On the arrival of Bhishma, the entire court stood in reverence and I could feel the blood boil under my very skin. The man who had destroyed my family on the name of his Dharma was worshipped by one and all for his valour and wisdom. His face reflected his staunch disapproval of the game. Being wise, he could understand that the game was a design to exploit the Pandavas. But what his wisdom could not see was that the game was a design to end him and the Kuru dynasty, altogether.

The Pandavas in their royal finery took their seats. Yudhishthira took his seat, opposite Duryodhana at the podium. An excited Duryodhana made the announcement, "My mama, Shakuni would be playing on my behalf, as I'm no match to Yudhishthira and would not make a worthy opponent". I could sense the air of disbelief in the Sabha. People murmured about Dharma and deceit, but no one dared to question the evil Duryodhana. They knew he would not spare naysayers. But Bhishma, objected, "This is not a fair arrangement, Duryodhana. We all know how skilled Shakuni is in the game, he would certainly defeat anyone." As flattering as it was, to hear my arch-rival speak highly of me, I retorted, "If Yudhishthira is afraid to play against me, he can say so and walk out of the game". This was enough to convince the gullible Yudhishthira. He agreed to play the game against me and my enchanted dice.

I knew this was the moment I was waiting for, my entire lifetime. I may never be able to avenge myself using my brawns, but isn't the fruit of revenge always sweet, despite the path taken to attain it? As I looked at the dice, I heard the faint voice of my father saying, "Do not forget the injustices meted out to us, dear Shakuni. You are the sole survivor of my 100 sons. The self-righteous Bhishma and the vile Dhritarashtra destroyed our family. Use the dice made out of my backbone at an opportune moment, I will roll at your command. You may not be able to dictate destiny, but you can certainly alter it with the enchanted dice".

As I looked at Bhishma, the horrendous past of my family flashed vividly before my eyes. My sister Gandhari had an inauspicious star in her horoscope which signified that she would be widowed by her first marriage. To avert such a misfortune, we married her to a goat and had it killed. Soon after, she was married to Dhritarashtra. But Bhishma, on finding that the bride of the royal family of Kuru was a widow, was furious. He imprisoned my father and my brothers in the ghastly towers of Hastinapura. He believed, if this news reached the ears of the neighbouring kingdoms, it would be a grave insult to the Kuru Dynasty. I questioned how a King marrying a widow would cause disrespect to the royal family. But Bhishma believed it was the Dharma of the Dwapara Yuga. "A Kshatriya, especially a King cannot be involved in such a marriage, at least publicly", he declared. He had starved my entire family to death, by offering minuscule amounts of food. My family decided to save me, to avenge the family's death and gave me their portions of the food as well. Shortly, my father also passed away and I, the sole male survivor of my family, was retrieved by the grace of Gandhari.

I was rudely brought back to the present by an impatient Duryodhana. As the game began, I decided to let Yudhishthira win the first few rounds to gain his trust and soothe his ego. The first few rounds, he won the wagered horses, royal finery and the crown jewels of Hastinapura. Like a fish to the worm, the trusting

Yudhishthira walked right into my trap. He got too involved in the game, to the dismay of his brothers.   And slowly, I began commanding my enchanted dice to roll the number, I needed. Soon, I had won his war elephants, horses, state coffers, the jewels and finery that the Pandavas were wearing. Sahadeva warned Yudhishthira, "Beloved Brother, I feel it's time for you to accept defeat and walk out of the game". There was a sense of foreboding in his voice. At this point, Uluka looked worriedly at me, but he knew not to interfere. He could not believe his father was dishonest with him.

Bhishma and Guru Dhronacharya looked disapprovingly at me. They knew I was not playing fair. But nobody knew the secret behind my dice. I taunted Yudhishthira, "A true Kshatriya warrior does not accept defeat unless he has truly lost all his wealth and property". He looked unperturbed and nodded at me to continue playing. Duryodhana beamed with joy, as he was winning against the Pandavas. He knew, soon he would own not just the Palace of Maya, in Indraprastha, but the Pandavas themselves.

I goaded Yudhishthira into wagering his four brothers. One after another, he kept losing each brother to Duryodhana. Finally, the four brothers were the servants/slaves of Duryodhana. I wanted to stop the game with this. I knew I had gravely offended the Pandavas and triggered fury in their minds. This would be reason enough for Yudhishthira, with the help of Krishna and his Yadava army to attack Hastinapura. He would destroy anyone on his path to retrieving his brothers from Duryodhana. This way, I would see the end of Bhishma and the dynasty that he held dear to him. I knew I would also lose my life, as I was Duryodhana's uncle. The thought of walking into the funeral pyre with Bhishma did not affect me. My father kindled the embers of revenge in my heart, I fed it passionately every day until it began consuming me entirely in its insatiable hunger, revenge and I became one.

The vile Duryodhana instigated Yudhishthira to wager himself. Before I could comment, Dhritarashtra had given his approval, "A Kshatriya warrior fights until he loses everything, Yudhishthira still has himself to wager", he bellowed. Yudhishthira then lost himself and his wife, Draupadi. She, along with the Pandavas had insulted Duryodhana in Indraprastha. Now, he wanted to avenge his insult.

It was then, at that very moment, I realized, just as I had used Duryodhana as a pawn, he had used me, all along, as well. The rest of the events of the day gained momentum like an avalanche. But I knew, it would only add more oil in the already blazing fire of the Pandavas. Before I knew it, Draupadi was dragged down to the court in front of the leering eyes of the Kauravas. She begged the elders in the gathering, "How could he wager away his wife, as if she were his property, especially after he wagered himself?" Someone in the court declared, according to Dharma, even a slave had the right to wager his wife. I knew Bhishma would not bat an eye, he would find solace in knowing he was not perpetrating any Adharma. This was the terrible fate of the brides of the Kuru dynasty, I thought. Duryodhana made gestures implying her to sit on his lap. I tried in vain to stop Duryodhana from what he was about to do.

I was no longer pulling the strings; Duryodhana only needed my help to create the moment; suddenly he took complete charge of the strings. I saw Dushasana, on the orders of Duryodhana, trying in vain to disrobe Draupadi, I saw her modesty being divinely protected, and I heard curses being hurled and vows being taken. I was a silent spectator of the events that uncoiled on account of my actions. Sahadeva's infuriated voice boomed across the Sabha, "I will be the end of Shakuni; I will kill him to avenge the dishonour of Draupadi". Undeterred, I knew I would never regret the destruction, I would cause, in the pursuit of my ambition and my vengeance.

I noticed Uluka's eyes glistening with tears. I knew I had fallen in his eyes; the image of his father was shattered in his heart. I wondered if he would still love me. But the only thing I needed him to know was that I was a warrior in my own right. I was courageous enough to live through the consequences of my actions. As his father, the only redemption I seek, from him, is to be acknowledged for the ambition and boundless passion, I exhibited in my life.

7

THE MACE

by Tipston Rubus

F irm and quiet steps resonated with the evening breeze and prattling of grass. Shadow of a chiselled young frame flashed over the dry barks of matured banyans, poplars, and neem as he padded swiftly along the fence. Hoping to lay a firm grip with bare hands on the tall fence, in a wink Duryodhana's clear face, broad shoulders, hard and perfectly shaped torso briefly gleamed in the evening sun before he jumped outside and sprinted towards the river into the jungle.

Duryodhana walked fast and his face expressed his enraged mind. Drona taught martial arts and warfare to him, along with his brothers and the Pandavas. Earlier that morning, everyone was designated a weapon that would befit their strength and calibre which they will master. Duryodhana had mastered the mace as much as Bhima. Drona chose the latter to be armed with the mace as he was fierce and physically the strongest. Displeased, Duryodhana challenged the pronouncement. It was immediately decided that the two contestants would wrestle and winner trains with mace.

Bhima had a huge physique owing to his gluttony. He bullied Duryodhana's brothers into handing over their food. They abided, as he otherwise would get them beaten up. As far as his relationship with Duryodhana, they'd always been the arch-nemesis of each other. Duryodhana preferred wearing coloured silk always, sometimes even in the wrestling ring. He had his hair oiled, combed, and well-groomed all day. Drona would chide "your attire shows pride, which is not a warrior's trait. You disregard the sanctity of this training". Duryodhana, however, shrugged off and carried on.

Bhima, who hated his guru being disrespected, would attempt to disrobe Duryodhana at the ring as they wrestle, but failed each time before the latter's agility and speed. A split second of loosening up was enough for Duryodhana to take advantage of his opponent in the ring. Besides, he was tricky with his unprecedented moves, sometimes hoodwink to win through. He had a stern control over his brothers, to have them cheer for him each time he contested a Pandava. He told them it showed Kauravas strength and unity while it was his strategy to distract and blow out the opponent's confidence. Hence Bhima resorted to tearing up his cousin's clothes and setting them on fire as they dried after laundry. Duryodhana still wouldn't stop getting them replaced with new ones.

The two walked into the ring amidst the cheer of their brothers, facing each other in their loincloths tied intact high above their knees, with Bhima slapping his trunk-like thigh. Duryodhana rubbed a handful of sand between his palms and clapped once forming a mild smoke of dust. As they took their stance with legs spread out and knees half bent, Drona signalled the dual to begin. In an instance, the two clasped hands and pushed each other. First, one to fall on his back loses claim for the mace. Duryodhana roared loud as Bhima stood unassailable. Each time Bhima reached for his opponent with one hand, Duryodhana would swiftly dodge. Meanwhile, it was a cakewalk for the former to release himself from the clutches of his combatant. Rapid foot movements, twists and turns formed a cloud of dust around the two.

Regretting that in spite of matching the strength of a thousand Elephants, his father lost claim to the throne due to his blindness, Duryodhana grew up with hostility towards the Pandavas. He urged to grow up to be a perfect man that no one would resist. Things hit hard when the royal teachers took a natural liking for the Pandavas over him and his siblings, turning him disregardful of his teachers. Out of envy, he would play pranks on his cousins imagining if one of them must be lethal to kill them all or blind them. Eventually, with more of such acts, he became infamous among the royal subjects. Now in the ring, he looked for a chance where he could blind Bhima with the tiny stones below his feet, or perhaps make him lame for tormenting his brothers. He told himself, "I want Bhima to yield, to see his brothers ashamed. Not pain, but in shame, they must scorn. I shall prove the Pandavas unworthy."

Bhima's every attempt to hold Duryodhana had failed in the meantime. The latter was cautious for he knew that Bhima's hold could be fatal. He already had Bhima's palm print on his bare chest and shoulders from all the smacking. Duryodhana's strategy was to exhaust his opponent before ambushing him. Precisely calculating Bhima's breath, he found the right time to strike a sweet spot on the former's shoulder to hold. The first strike went in vain as Duryodhana was swung, pushed aside landing on his knee while Bhima towered, impregnable.

"Only more weight on one of his shoulders would bring him down", thought Duryodhana.

In a jiffy, he pounced back as hard as he could, clutching Bhima's shoulder and neck he swung around, landing hard on his thigh with his adversary falling on his back to bite the dust. The Kauravas hooted and praised their brother, while the Pandavas stood shocked and crestfallen. Duryodhana relished the ovation.

"This is an outrage!", Drona bellowed. The crowd went silent as everyone turned to their guru, who glowered at Duryodhana, "you landed on your thigh".

"I won", the Kaurava prince sounded pompous.

According to dharma, the laws, and ethics of warfare one is supposed to land on their feet or knee in the move Duryodhana used. "This is anarchy. You failed to follow the Dharma", Drona bawled.

"Only the weak follow Dharma", Duryodhana scoffed turning to the Pandavas, "the mighty shall be judicious to win."

"Dharma is meant to protect the mighty while they grow mightier. That will only make you frail", Drona pointed at Duryodhana's thigh. "One who disregards the dharma shall not wield a mace. Bhima will train with it."

"Pain shall be a worthy price I pay for my victories", Duryodhana walked away from the ring, in fuming strides. In the evening he sneaked out and had reached the river.

The river flowed cutting through a dense jungle. It was wide enough to hold a ship and deep for five full-grown elephants to sink in one over the other. Duryodhana had come there for archery lessons. It was in that same spot where he stood, a few days ago they encountered a tribal boy of their age, Ekalavya. He was a self-taught archer who learned from eavesdropping into Drona's classes, yet mastered the art better than Arjuna. His arrows hit targets Arjuna could not think of. He had made a disfigured effigy of Drona and spread offerings before it. It was only lumps of mud piled to look like a human body, in which Ekalavya saw Drona. Duryodhana thought, "this must be the most anyone could like this man".

On contrary, Drona was displeased at a low born excelling warfare. He could not let down the dharma he believed in. In return for being his guru, Drona asked for a pay. He said, "Give me your right thumb in return for the knowledge I've imparted". Ekalavya was taken aback by the demand, as he did not expect it. Duryodhana yearned the request to be denied, but the tribal boy, believing that archery was a Kshatriya's skill, cut off his thumb and submitted it with devotion at Drona's feet, who was very careful about not touching it.

Duryodhana felt a sharp pang of disappointment as Drona denied him the mace, citing the same dharma which blemished a skilled archer at that very spot. He felt his pain resonated with Ekalavya's, hence ran down to find him. He saw a ruined hut and Drona's effigy marred, but the boy was nowhere to be found. Duryodhana stood looking at the river without blinking an eye, taking deep breaths, his lips mumbled, and eyes teared up vexed and angry.

Years rolled by. It was the day of the annual warfare contest between the Pandavas and Kauravas. With Dhritarashtra, the blind king and his queen Gandhari, King Pandu and his queen Kunti assumed their seats in the balcony. The royal teachers Kripa and Drona sat along with Bhishma to judge the contest. The humongous gallery was fully packed. It was the event Hastinapura eagerly awaits each year, to see Bhima's strength, Arjuna's precision, Duryodhana's agility and spectacle of talents from every Pandava and Kaurava prince. The entire kingdom had left their personal affairs aside, rushed to witness the grandeur, skill, and valour. Winners were presented with titles and honours by the judges in the name of the king.

Duryodhana sat alongside his maternal uncle Shakuni, who was known as his political mentor. Shakuni had a shared dislike for the Pandavas with Duryodhana. As Bhima displayed his strength by lifting a huge rock above his head, Shakuni commented, "Might help him carry his brothers someday" and they laughed together. Duryodhana always knew that his uncle had a prolonged hatred for his cousins, for he too thought that only the Dharma protected the Pandavas, if not for which they would have long gone. Shakuni had a disturbing past where he lost all that he held closer which had to be avenged. Although Duryodhana was aware of it, he chose not to doubt his uncle.

Arjuna always performed last as everyone present was aware that his was the most sought-after part of the entire event. The crowd cheered and hooted as he walked up to the arena. Some had brought flower petals to hurl on him. The crowd adored Arjuna as they considered him the best archer in the world. Duryodhana remained unmoved as he imagined a teenage tribal boy among all these applause instead of Arjuna. The subjects, however, thought he envied his cousin. Arjuna began his display by hitting the bull's eye of a target board placed in the far end of the gallery. He moved on to hit multiple targets in all directions, which shifted to moving targets. He shot sixty-three arrows in a minute, which was the most number of arrows drawn in that span of time in all the world.

As soon as his display was complete, Bhishma ran up to Arjuna, held his shoulders to congratulate him. Drona and Kripa gave him a standing ovation. "I am proud to have taught the best archer of all times", Drona boastfully laughed. Kripa added, "There are a few warriors who hold on to the values of the Dharma, all of them invincible and so is Arjuna". As words of praise kept coming in on Arjuna, Duryodhana grew restless worried by his inability to prove them wrong. Just then a beaming voice quietened the crowd. "Stop!"

A young man, long-haired, tall and striking, jumped over the barricade separating the gallery from the ring and walked towards Arjuna. He wore a golden armour that added up to his might. "This is merely blowing your own trumpet", he said in a seething tone. Contesting the decision, he asked the jury to allow him to display his skills in archery. "I shall prove you all wrong", he uttered with confidence.

"Who are you?" Kripa walked forward.

"Karna", the young man spoke loud and clear.

"Are you a Kshatriya? Who is your father? And your lineage?", Karna stood stunned by these questions from Kirpa. He lowered his head and the crowd burst out laughing

"I was a student of Drona", Karna stuttered.

"That doesn't answer me", Kripa mocked. Drona got up, "Karna. Unaware of his lineage, he is the adopted son of Adhiratha, the charioteer". The crowd erupted aloud laughing again.

"You know not of your lineage, nothing of your birth and above all raised by a charioteer. What more shame can you be born with? This place and archery are for warriors, for Kshatriyas; not low borns like you. This is no child's play", Kripa sneered at Karna.

"I doubt if it is a child's play unless I get my turn to show my skills", Karna laughed.

Duryodhana sat astonished to see what unfurled before him. He walked front "His confidence deserves a chance. Go ahead Karna show us what you have".

Karna aced all the tests as good as Arjuna. He matched Arjuna by shooting 63 arrows in a minute. Birds were used as moving targets in the contest. Archers were asked to put their arrow through on part of the bird. While Arjuna was asked to aim for its heart, Kirpa asked Karna to go for its head. "I shall hit it in the eye", Karna said. He took aim and struck it right through the eye. The crowd applauded like never before, for they had never imagined one among them would do it. To Duryodhana it was reminiscent of Ekalavya again, "but this one would not cut off his finger", he thought.

"Arjuna! This is not it. I will show things you might not have seen if you can step forward", Karna called. Arjuna agreed, "Let's do this eye to eye".

Kripa interrupted, "Arjuna! You are a Kshatriya. Only another of your kind can challenge you for a dual. Karna! Leave."

Just then, seeing Karna left speechless, Duryodhana stood up. "Is this how your dharma regards talent? How can one's valour be judged by his birth? We witnessed Karna put an arrow through the eye of a bird. Is that not a skill? We carry weapons cast-off iron into war and not that made of butter. Most of our royal teachers who train warriors are not Kshatriya. Does Dharma explain it?"

"You can't question us. We are above all that we determine Dharma" Kripa answered. Only a Kshatriya can wield a weapon, be a warrior and king. Only he can challenge Arjuna. That is Dharma", Kripa shouted enraged.

"So be it", Duryodhana stated, "If only a king shall challenge Arjuna, From now on Karna is a king. I present to you Karna, a friend, a warrior and the new king of Anga". Duryodhana felt complacent. He had saved another thumb from being cut off.

8

A SCARLET LOVE

by Ruchka Gulati

The valances burgundy threw a richness of aged velvet in faded sheen. Royal colours speak of bygone lores lost in time. The fringes on the curtain gathered in perfect harmony- with no eloquence denied. Two tie backs in auric splendour aided to part the curtains a little to give a glimpse of the manicured garden and patterned parterre of urban stones. Certainly, a walk in the garden was a delight of varied hues, wafting smell and fluttering butterflies that lingered to sigh, upon this sight. A true paradise that breathed the glory of yore. Settling my mind back to the ballroom where my whispered words would echo, I stilled beneath a chandelier in red Turkish crystals skilfully hand cut. To say it was opulent would be less as the richness of its colour sparked from every candlelight that twinkled upon sight and it hung over a major part of the floor of pure teak burnished and sleek. Reflections of all fell on it as a mirage. A cordoned area marked with a Sign X caught my eye. The didactic wall panel gave details of the varied exhibits in the ballroom of this stately home, with text entailing dates, sketchy history. This was dated as the scene of a passionate crime which I relived with the headphones buzzing words. The story was detailed and expanded more in the estate's educators manual. What invoked curiosity was a slim booklet titled 'A love lore' with a subtext that read 'of deceit and passion.'

I took a bench lined beside and sat to read.

***

Anna Natalia Drewkosky

Lord Elbertstone IV

Dated 21st June 1889

Bluemead House, famous for its Elbertstone Hall, English Gardens, The Headstone Library.

The sun grabbed her face and cupped it in its palm, warmth coursed through sans sunscreen lapped face, it was a golden burnished brown beautiful to the obscure eye. Her slim hands lifted to twirl her vagabond black hair into a rough bun, askew. A few strands escaped as if to beckon freedom to question her audacity to curb, she relinquished a desire to tuck them into place and with a resigned sigh overlapping grit and determination, walked on. Her resolve made, she could not linger more or procrastinate- that was an intrinsic part of her demeanour. Anna had to bare her thoughts and tell all.

She walked in stoic silence the burden of the lie raw and biting on her shoulders. It hurt her every awakened moment. It weighed her down and she felt her neck twinge with the pain of recall. Unknowingly her fingers lifted to rub the nape of her neck as if it would ease the jangled nerves. She had lied like a Cretan and now she bore the burden of it on her bony clavicle. She hoped for penance or retribution of sorts, which gave reason for this long walk to freedom with measured steps.

A church beyond two ubiquitous buildings marked her destination. Her feet saddled in sandals flat, simplicity defined, were perfect for this trudge on paved pedestrian walks through marked lanes and alleys that her synapses had marked. She did not need to apply her mind to the mundane as grave things of consequence needed attention as she traversed this journey to salvation. Fear leaves indelible marks on our psyche and evokes actions that cajole the senses. Her daily routine was an act defined by her god-fearing nature. Her belief allayed that sins committed needed redemption and God would grant relief. This simple doctrine governed her existence and actions. So, freedom to commit came with an underlying assurance that if you commit a sin, God in his court can aid with salvaging you from the misdeeds. Or at least Anna assumed this. She survived her days with fallacy and minor aberrations formed around her nature at free will.

Anna heaved a sigh as she saw the pentacle on the spire. The precinct of the All Saints Cathedral paved a way for hope and release. She walked towards the ambulatory and lit a vigil candle, she watched it burn with a flicker warm and consoling and sat with subdued melancholy but with salvation in mind. The prie-dieu felt her aching words as she whispered her confession.....

'I carried the weight on my shoulders, forgive me for I did lie.' She paused briefly and continued.

'God, salvage my body from this inferno of passion and love.' Her lips trembled and a tear slipped involuntarily.

'Forgive me for I sinned.'

'A moment of insanity, a moment of passion, born to the moment, was my guilty pleasure.' She stopped, her voice constricted lower by two decibels.

'I have broken vows to love him forever and given my wanton desires to another.' She rushed with the last words to usher them out and release. She squeezed her eyes tighter and in abated silence waited... waited for a sign, an indication, a halo to appear before, that may bespeak and bless her aching heart or ease her turmoil. Anna did hope for much. Not knowing that healing is just in believing and not in the act of redemption revealing. The mind fights battles and overcomes as the mind is powerful when powered.

Was a miracle to happen now? Would God now take over and tell Elbert of her amorous dalliance? Anna did so imagine this. Belief creates miracles and emboldens you to fight and surpass challenges which else wise would seem insurmountable. She certainly needed conviction by her side.

She walked leaving the silence of the church with a smile. She felt light and carefree again. The sun seemed brighter and merrier in her eye.

Elbert sat as emotions racked his mind. He paced a few steps as anger assailed then sat clenching fists. He saw no reasoning- for him, this was a betrayal. His love was not driven by passion alone as women in plenty waded through seeking him out. His one smile made many swoon. In Anna, he found an allure of simplicity, humility, and a beauty she was unaware of. Her slender form and long black tresses with kiss-curls around her cheeks drew glances and Elbert would have loved to gorge those eyes out. Those barbaric thoughts probably spoke of strains in his genes he could not avoid. When love becomes a raging passion that blinds your vision, it can be detrimental too. Elbert's love had a furious passionate streak and sometimes bordered in violent expulsions. He lavished her with precious jewels, ornaments that would adorn her. For he knew nothing about love. In his eyes love was showering with packaged surprises of expensive kinds, love did not play a role beyond the ardour of the act. His definition of love defied love. What was love? It did not mean sacrifice or the kind that made a soul cry with amorous longings or a heart warm with beautiful feelings. Love for this man was a new creature who he did not know. A child molly-coddled grows with feelings that soften the mind and teaches the delicate nuances of loving and growing and they imbibe with the observation of matrimony or happy exchanges lent through parenting examples. He stood deprived. Anna suffered from an inadequacy that lent reasons to her acceptance of it all. Her insecurities masked, lay deep-rooted to childhood. She was a lone child to destiny born. She survived each night praying that her father would not get abusive. Her father returned home every night in a drunken stupor and her mother and she bore the brunt. The scars stayed even after their death. She has lived in aloneness. To her love was, basking in the arms of her lover, tied to vows of forever. Anna was in love with the thought of love and illusions that were far from reality. A daydreamer, who stayed awake weaving tales of 'lived happily ever after' in varied forms. Her imagination stayed to become her hopeful reality. Reality is strange and far removed and sometimes stranger than fiction. She suffered denials that racked her dreams. She saw silhouettes of matrimony in her naked walls, imagined sitting by the fire on a cold winter eve watching the dying embers. A husband beside with glances of love and children sleeping in the warmth of the cosy cot.

She waited for a ring to tie her heart. Elbert gave none and her sighs flew out of the window and dreams lay shattered. This was not enough; all was not in her destiny. In a moment of rage mingled with despair, she had wandered into the arms of another and here a new tale began of lust and hope for a future. A rich paramour with promises laced in every spoken word was dreams coming true.

Lord Elbertstone, needed no introduction

Bequeathed with a legacy of estates, a villa in Russia, Chateau in Italy, stretching gardens one was flanked by soft rolling hillocks that boast of a view of the city below. A gated mansion where he chose to reside and called it home. His parents had died in an untimely car accident. It had stripped him of a normal childhood and gentle parenting. It threw him headlong into challenges he could not have perceived. Elbert to the keen eye suffered from a life of riches but without love and for many years avoided relationships till Anna crossed his path. A perfect love story but ever after was denied. His guardian had left a will that said that he must marry a woman of chosen status or give all up.

The legalities burdened and bound him.

I paused here to imagine Elbert in this palatial stately home with sprawling gardens and wondered where this tale was going. Intriguing as the characters unfolded on my lap, where I cradled this book. Strangely there were gaps here as Anna's years of bliss or details of Elbert in the years between were lost. No yellowing pages of history bore testimony to that. An anomaly that made me feel sad. The story straight cuts to Anna the famed Ballerina. Sketchy but left my imagination playing into their story.

Chapter 9

Dated 8th March 1892

Anna woke up elated today was her famed performance at a masquerade ball. She gathered her tutu and packed her ballerina shoes and all the required ensemble in a duffel bag and cross-checked her do list. Then with a glance at her face in the mirror before leaving she closed the door.

There was a car waiting for her. She sat in the car and inhaled the smell of rich leather seats and leaned back to close her eyes. She so needed a brief moment of quiet. She opened them as the chauffeur braked suddenly and broke her reverie. now they were driving up a gentle slope and slowly leaving the city lights behind. Silver oak, English birch, aspen and varied flowering trees beautifully lined the driveway. At a distance, she saw the Bluemead House. The facade concealed until you approached the cobblestone driveway.

The valet took her bag and guided her to a room. She was served English tea and warm scones with clotted cream and asked to relax and make herself comfortable.

The masquerade ball was marked by a plaque exquisitely encased and border carved with gold leaf. Below it was an ornate onyx table atop that an embellished book, a mother of pearl inlaid box, velvet lined with a gold-tipped pen. She was guided to the ballroom for her performance in the masquerade ball. The ballroom, where all state functions were held now privately owned had an exclusive entry too. The owner's name was kept secret under privacy laws. It was simply beautiful.

The burgundy valances a richness threw. The walls were adorned by cameo gold-leafed and intaglio friezes of figurines. The pendant lights threw a shadow on the walls. The ceiling engraved beautifully was for its most part concealed by a chandelier that threw red from its candle lights. The guest list boasted of lords of manors ladies of status, from an echelon of society considered regal. They in their regalia graced the occasion. The hall went abuzz with excitement when they announced her arrival and this was the moment much anticipated by all.

Clothed as Kouros, but by design, In a mask of pure gold intricately carved by the best craftsmen from Venice that concealed much. The dominion stood in the shadows of a passage lined by Gothic pillars. His sinister gaze, a mocking smile stole his face. He stealthily slipped a quick glance and patted his concealed revolver. His head throbbed with a strange excitement of revenge and his sense stood as if devoured by it all. He had planned all meticulously. Yes, all for years. Patience was his virtue. Planning was his acquired skill and blind passion was inherited. He mingled all.

The ballerina in her pink tutu stilled when she looked into a pair of eyes a deep-sea blue. How could she forget them? Those eyes in which she had drowned all her caring; those eyes that graced her heart; those deep pools now held a glazed look, vengeful, hatred filled, and they belonged to Elbert. She saw it all- lost love had stolen the warmth and instead flecks of fury remained. Recognition brought trepidation and that dragged fear and sent a chill through her spine. It happened all in a split second. A bullet sailed to pierce her wanton heart, and another split her skull apart. Blood poured as if from a chalice and Anna fell crumpled, in a bloodthirsty cluster of pain, her mangled heart rained red. Tears escaped from her eyes mingled with the incarnadine and streaked her bloody cheeks.

The crystal lights shattered, fell and glass shards scattered freely. Red crystals in all their rich glory soaked in ruby red blood thickened with lust. A pandemonium broke loose. Strangled muted cries, shrieks and wails, carcasses strewn on an erstwhile splendid floor. Blood dried as hatred dried. Humans laid low in a blood bath, killed as venom drained from him. Lord Elbertstone still with the smoking weapon in his hand but unveiled. His face and anguish stroked his trembling cry as he kneeled before the body of Anna and stared devoid of thoughts, caressed her cheek, and lifted his blood embalmed hands and paled. A new glaze of terror and loss surfaced. He stayed like that till he was surrounded by authorities and taken away.

A berserk mind, deranged, demented sows seeds of hate. Melancholia steals sanity and a frenzied mind plays into the hand of psychosis.

To his defence, Elbert said 'Mea Culpa,' I admit.

His face contorted with anguish.

'I killed her.'

'I loved her,' with this he cried.

'Her betrayal was my living death. I staged this massacre. For riches I hate.' His hands tightly fisted, sweaty, he continued…

'In a moment of insanity, a moment of passion, a moment of hatred, a moment of revenge, I killed'. He bemoans as all is lost. He is secluded and curses himself. His heart cried with the pain of sorrow and lachrymal tears nursed his soul.

'Sadly, in life.' the judge said.

'This is the knell of mankind's mind. When we let hatred and revenge stay in it.'

'Non-compos mentis.' pronounced the jury.

Not of sound mind and thus not responsible for his actions.

9

LOVE FOR THE GAME

by Uma Bokil

Delhi

Samar

I hated the din of the club. The bass was making my head throb, and hordes of people huddled together in such close proximity were making me claustrophobic. For the umpteenth time, I felt glad about having gotten a floor for private dining and booths built above this zoo. The club would soon go, too, and then, I wouldn't have to witness these good-for-nothing children wasting their lives in booze and the after-effects of their hangovers. This place could benefit with some class.

Joe caught up to me, his eyes constantly darting in every direction, and the rest of his skittle dolls in black uniforms enveloped me from all sides, like always.

"Six missed calls from Sehgal. Again," he said.

"Any message saying what he wants?"

Joe smirked. "Sehgal and texting? Really?"

I chuckled and tried to bee-line my way to the dining above, but college groupies had blocked the entrances of both the staircases leading upstairs. Just as I struggled to ascend one, I heard catcalls and hooting from the dance arena. Swivelling my head around to my right, I halted. Suddenly, the chaos didn't matter. I could neither hear the bass, nor the deafening noise people these days called music; nor could I breathe. All I could do was stare agape at her.

She was dressed provocatively in red, her dress just the right amount of short that it didn't make her look indecent, yet enough to show off her slender, toned legs. She was swaying to the music alone. I'd never seen a person look so complete in their mere existence. She was moving vivaciously and sensually, occasionally moving her hands through her hair, as if she were under a spell, intoxicated by her own vibrancy, and I were a mere fragment caught up in her resonance.

I moved towards her, suddenly wishing it were my hands moving through her hair, holding her, caressing her. She noticed me making my way over to her, and I was so focused on her face that I could even see her mouth curl up into a smirk from afar. The smirk widened as I closed off the distance, and she sashayed her hips flirtatiously.

With ease, I slipped my arm around her perfect waist, pulling her close to me. Our noses touching, we gazed at each other's lips, hers stunningly bow-shaped and full. Her eyes carried a sweet yet lustrous dominance. The only thing that broke the hex I seemed to be under was the song slowly fading out to an end.

"Liked what you saw?" She smiled seductively, her eyes boring into mine.

"If you'd join me, I'd show you just how much."

She looked at me quietly for a minute, worrying me that she'd say no.

"I'd like that," she said at last, and I caught myself sighing in relief.

I guided her back to where my men were waiting, and we climbed upstairs. Finally nestling in a booth far off in a corner, Joe and his squad scattered around the place to engage security.

Making herself at home, she ordered a whiskey, neat, while I asked for a Scotch on the rocks with a twist.

"Well, not that I'd mind calling you 'gorgeous' all night, but I'd love to know your name," I said, casually wrapping my arm around the seat.

"Who said I was going to be here all night?"

I blinked at her, at a loss for words. Why did I say that?

"I'm kidding!" she laughed. "Oh, the look on your face."

My insides swooned at the sound of her laugh.

"I'm Zeya," she said finally. She smiled again, but this time, it had a warmth that made me stare at her all over again.

"And you?" she asked.

"Excuse me?"

"What's your name?"

Two of my men who were within earshot whisked their heads in our direction, faces contorted with flabbergast. That was a question I hadn't been asked in a couple of years.

"I –"

"You look so cute when you're shocked," she laughed again. "You're Samar Ahuja, CEO and Founder of Ahuja's Designs, the renowned Interior Design Consultancy firm. You bought this club, turned it into a chic restaurant, and are one of the youngest self-made billionaires in the country." She winked. "I read a lot." Her eyes sparkled.

I grinned. Who was this woman?

We engaged in an easy flow of conversation over drinks, and I found myself intrigued by her with each passing minute.

"So, Zeya, what do you do?"

"I'm a lawyer," she replied simply. "Although, I do love partying."

I turned to her. "Then I assume you know all the right places."

"Yes. Why?"

"According to you, what would make a club the hotspot for the elite public? Take the club downstairs for example."

"What made you ask?" She questioned.

"I've renovated a lot of places, but clubs are my debut. I thought I'd dive into the public eye. Sometimes, the best things are too obvious to the eye to be noticed."

"Well, let's see. I'd lose the DJ, get a live band, keep the dance floor, make this an exclusive membership-only club, and extend a dining downstairs for formal dinners and cocktail parties. Oh, and the interior desperately needs a change. This place could use some class."

I took her to bed.

***

A week later, I was heading out to work when my phone rang.

"On my way, Mr. Sehgal. Yes. No, don't do anything unless I get there. Uh-huh. Okay." I quickly hung up. I read the email I received the previous afternoon from one of our top investors for the tenth time.

Herman and Co. had been one of our investors since ages. They had recently planned an employee retreat at my resort in Miami which had gone horribly awry. Apparently, the hospitality and management were abhorrent, and room service was like a B&B, both of which I found implausible. And now, they wanted to sue.

I arrived at The Greene Hotel at five minutes to noon for my lunch appointment with Sehgal.

"Reservation under Mr. Sehgal," I told the maître d'.

"Right this way, Mr. Ahuja. Mr. Sehgal is already here."

Sehgal looked years older than I'd seen him last. Cancer was never a good thing. After a handshake and a brief hug, we ordered lunch and cut to the chase.

"Get this. Herman and Co.'s accusations are way over the line." Sehgal began.

"Thought so," I murmured. "So, what exactly did happen?"

"One of the waiters spilled a drink on one of their employees during an important dinner. Sometime later, the same waiter stumbled while serving dessert and spilled hot chocolate sauce on three people. A lady was furious because the hot sauce reddened her skin. Also, apparently, our Thai massage facility didn't exactly feel Thai."

I groaned. "Get us out of this, please."

"I will. On one condition."

"Which is?"

He gave me the same sheepish look which I'd come to recognize since quite some time. Realization dawned upon me.

"Mr. Sehgal, you know I respect you and your daughter must be really beautiful but –"

"Please, just meet her. I invited her over. She's your age, pretty, smart – you know, like me."

I couldn't help but smile.

"All the same, I really wish you hadn't –"

"Dad?" said a familiar voice.

Sehgal's gaze moved past me and he smiled warmly. Turning around in my chair, my jaw dropped as I stared unblinkingly, disbelievingly at none other than Zeya. Grinning, she walked to our table. She was dressed in formals, looking stunning, completely contrast to the woman I'd met at the club, and yet, so alluring.

"Hi, I'm Zeya." She extended her hand.

I gaped at her, dumb-founded.

"Told you she was pretty," Sehgal smiled. "Anyway, you kids catch up. I need to use the restroom."

I kept smiling till Sehgal was out of sight, then turned back to her.

"You're Zeya Sehgal?"

"Guilty," she smiled sheepishly. "Speaking of, could you not tell him we've already met?"

"Wow, was the night that bad?"

She swatted my arm playfully. "You're too much. No, he'd go crazy if he heard that his daughter was doing a "come have me" kind of dance in a club, only to have been taken by his client."

We talked for a while till Sehgal returned. He looked expectantly between the two of us. "Well?"

I looked at Zeya, who was smiling secretly, and then cleared my throat.

"Mr. Sehgal, Zeya's a lovely woman. If you allow me, I'd love to take her out to dinner this weekend."

Zeya's smile lit up the room.

***

It's been two years since then. After we began dating exclusively, Mr. Sehgal was the happiest. A year ago, he succumbed to his cancer and passed away. Zeya took it hard.

Today, it's our anniversary. I take her to the same club where we had first met, which, thanks to Zeya, is now a classy place, and the rooftop of the building has turned into another fine dining. I take

Zeya up there, blindfolded. She takes off the blindfold to a view of the rooftop decorated with vanilla orchids and fairy lights, her favourite. The Way You Look Tonight plays softly in the background.

"Samar, this is –"

"Marry me."

"What?"

"Zeya, I was normal and happy before I met you. But now, I'm happier, jollier, everything a bit more than I used to be. And I love being that way. I want to see your gorgeous eyes looking into no one else's but mine every morning. I want to be the one to make your morning coffee, your whiskey neat; I want to be the man for you. Will you marry me?"

"Yes," she smiles.

***

Six months later

Zeya

I gaze outside the window. Honeymooning in Switzerland is mesmerizing. Samar has gone down to the reception to arrange for a private lunch up in the mountains in a secluded cabin. It's funny how having money can get you things you wouldn't have otherwise even afforded.

I load my revolver and keep it stacked out of view. I check my ticket to Italy and keep it well hidden along with my weapon. Eight hours before I reunite with Bijoy. I smile at the thought of him.

I hear the front door of our suite open, and I hide the bag in my big suitcase.

"Love? I got us the cabin. I just need to pay half the amount in advance."

"That's great, sweetie."

He switches on his laptop. Fifteen minutes pass by, and I can see him struggling.

"That's weird," he murmurs and makes a call. "Yes, hi, this is Samar Ahuja and I'm having trouble accessing my savings. It says my account balance is nil. Yes, that would help. Thank you." He hangs up and looks at me. "They're looking into it."

In less than a minute, he gets a call again. "Hi. Yes. No, that can't be right. No, it was jointly owned by Mr. Sehgal and me. No, he's no more. Well, he was bad with memory, so everything important must have been stored someplace safe. What are you talking about? I didn't transfer all the money to Sehgal and Associates. No, after his death, it all went to –"

He pauses. My back is to him, but I can picture his expression.

"Zeya?"

"Yes, darling?"

I turn around to face him, revolver in hand.

"It was so easy, getting all the passwords and documents from him. Love can be such a twisted game," I smile, gently caressing the revolver in my palms.

He stares at me, shocked. "I –"

"You look so cute when you're shocked," I sneer.

Three bullets shoot out and pierce his chest.

I open the dossier on Bijoy and take a last look – Bijoy Sharma, 28, owner of Miriam's Resorts, listed as one of the top ten billionaires of India. I chuckle and walk out of the room, excitement bubbling in my veins. The next pawn is waiting.

10

CHANDRANAKHA

by Radhika Menon

She listened to the forest and made her way towards the voices, her dark skin glistening in the sunlight seeping through the wild canopy. Her feet were accustomed to the forest. Her eyes darted from side to side. She could hear them better now. Strangers in the forest! She peeked through the bushes. There they were. Two men and a woman. They were unlike any other people she had ever laid eyes upon. "What brings such creatures here?", she mused.

One of them turned to look at her hiding place and they all fell silent. She felt her heart stop.

***

Like a ripple, she let the memory slowly move in her, finding a way to her chest. She clutched her left bosom, and a sharp pain brought her back. The sun had set. She pulled her veil closer to her and slowly began walking again. She had to find shelter. Soon it'll be dark. She did not want to fan the fears of the poor villagers further. She quickened her pace. She reached the woods at the northern end of the village and found the tallest tree. With surprising agility, she climbed the tree and stretched her limbs on a thick branch. She had climbed countless trees when she was a little girl. "Chandranakha! Chandranakha!", her mother would call out to the jungle. She would try hard to suppress her giggles as she watched her mother look for her everywhere from the top of the tree. She smiled fondly at the memory and slowly drifted off to sleep.

***

She found herself running with the wind. She was laughing. He was close at her heels. She turned to look at him and found herself in his arms. They laughed together for a while, immersed in their rendezvous.

"Vidyutjiva, my Love. We have to let my brother know of us. I can't bear to be away from you..", she breathed. "Soon. You know your brother better than anyone. I have to be ready. He will slay me the moment he sets his eyes on me."

"The times are changing, my brother would not disapprove of my choices, Vidyutjiva!"

"Patience, Chandranakha! Our time shall come"

***

She had woken up by dawn, her ears attuned to the faint humming of the birds waking up from their slumbers. She resumed walking, her feet slowly taking her to the faint gurgle of a waterfall. The water looked clean and dark, with the sunlight bouncing off its tiny waves. She set down her rucksack and lifted the veil off her face. She saw a pair of brown eyes, once long and tender, now severe and vacant, looking at her. She let those eyes travel, from her matted brownish hair to the place where her nose should've been, then to the sides of her head where her ears should have held her veil in place.

She untwined her weary form from the dirty rag and stepped into the water, slowly pulling it along with her. She let her hands travel to her neck, as she bent her head down to get a better look of the water plants that tickled her calloused feet. As she brought her palms further below, she smiled to herself at the price she had paid for confessing love. The jagged edges of regrown flesh that remained as a memory, sometimes haunting her with ghosts of her motherhood. The water flowed, with little leaps of joy as if dancing to the whispers of a faraway breeze. The little forest beings were not afraid of her, she was akin to them, though from a land so far away. The bees fluttered in harmony amidst the earth scented leaves. In the shade of the boughs, she waded in, watching the brief crescents of white in the water as the afternoon sun put the jungle in a slumber. Her eyes travelled downstream, down another memory lane, and for a moment, she wondered if she was at home. Home, where the jungle in her grew in all its glory, with her mother Kaikesi planting the seeds of everything in her.

***

She steadied her pace. The swim had brought back the green in her. She had a long way to go. Janaki's words kept ringing in her ears. "We are but possessions. That's all we ever were. It all happened because one man scorned another's possession. it has been happening since time immemorial and it will happen .."

***

Her maids had come rushing to the chambers. She had been summoned by her brother. Her brother, the one hailed Lankapati, feared and revered in all the three worlds. Her doting brother. She hurried, bubbling with excitement. It was with great effort that she convinced her brother to let Vidyutjiva accompany him. She wanted them to get along well. A thousand questions danced in her mind.

Her maids did not share her enthusiasm, nor did they try to keep in pace with her eager footsteps. It was only after a few moments that the feeling of unease pooled at the bottom of her heart. Something was amiss. The court lacked the commotion that accompanies after every hunting. She was ushered to her brother's chambers.

He was stretched in his bed, with the royal physician by his side. Mandodari, his wife stood by his feet, with unshed tears.

Her brother was injured. He looked weary as if he had aged overnight. They say pain does that to you.

"Who did this?", she whispered. No one had spoken a word. They stood there with downcast eyes. He opened his eyes and gestured to her to come closer. The hurt in his eyes bled more than the one in his chest.

She knew then, she was the reason this had happened. The ties of loyalty and the fervours of love forged by Vidyutjiva was but a farce to end the mighty Lankapati.

After dark, her dagger sat precariously on her skin. The harsh metal should have been cold and raw against her bare skin, but she could not feel anything except for the excruciating pain of his betrayal. She was just a pawn for him, as he readied himself for the war between Danavas and the Asuras. He would have made his way around the Pataal Lok thrice by now.

She did not hear the footsteps of Mandodari, nor did she feel the dagger being snatched away from her grasp and her son Shimbri placed on her lap.

That night, she had walked out of the fortress, to the forests where she knew she need not fear. No animal would strike her with betrayal, ever. No one had stopped her.

***

She hadn't known hunger since the war, only thirst. Yet, she fed herself a few wild berries. The swim had quenched her thirst. Penance had taught her to master human weaknesses, it was rumoured. "How ironic!", she mused. Shaking off her gnawing thoughts, she decided it was time to resume her journey.

The soft susurration of the branches, the loam in the earth and the petrichor of the decay filled her senses. She walked along a narrow path, which was uneven by the knotted roots that crossed it, branched at intervals. The path winded drearily.

***

She felt her heart stop. She had not known this sense ever. She willed her heart to beat as she looked at whom she thought to be the most beautiful person she had laid eyes upon. The time came to a stop. She had to know him. She hadn't moved from the spot. He heard the rustling of leaves from the bushes. He neared her hideaway, where she stood rooted.

"Laxman! What did you see?"

"Nothing brother! I thought I saw something", he called back as he retreated.

So that's his name. Laxman.

She found herself smiling, a feat she thought impossible after everything that had happened.

***

She opened her eyes. She had fallen asleep as she had paused for a while to catch her breath. Years of exhaustion was catching up to her. Her sister had begged her not to go. But she had to do this alone. After all, it is her head that holds the weight of the blame. The blame of bringing destruction to Lanka. The blame of inciting wrath in her brother that ultimately brought him, the unvanquishable Ravana, his death.

And she had been wearing it like a crown, all these years.

She resumed walking.

***

She had spent hours trying to know him from the branches, among the bushes, even under the gurgling waters of the river as he sat down to meditate by its bank. With each passing day, she felt it was fate that had brought him to the forests, and that her heart is going to be at the right place with him. She spent days training herself to let him know of her heart, she tried to master the way the woman with them talked.

***

The thick jungle canopy had slowly been pulled back, revealing clear blue skies curtained by bright gleams of sunlight. She found the land strangely barren. A contemptuous smile slowly began to form at her lips. A kingdom ruled by dharma. What dharma shall prevail in a land where the womb is scorned? Her meeting with the woman Janaki had gone unlike she had ever imagined. She felt she was talking to yet another Chandranakha, who was scorned and abandoned but strangely thought it was the way things have been and it is the way it will be.

***

She had approached them at daybreak that day.

"I am Chandranakha, the Princess of Lanka. The unvanquishable Ravana is my brother. I have fallen in love with you. Would you take me for your wife?", she spoke, not a trace of fear in her voice.

"I am but a slave to my brother. I have to ask him before I do anything. I think you should ask him, so we could have a marriage as you desire. "

She had pressed her request to his brother, Rama, as his wife stood watching, silently.

The details seemed blurry to her now. All she remembered was his mocking laughter as he cut off parts of her, her nose as she had the audacity to rise above her place and cast her eyes on him; her ears as a reminder and her breasts as atonement for her sinful mind as a lecherous soul.

She woke up to her brother's face.

***

The cawing of crows and the deep rumble followed by the sound of the crashing waves was heard at a distance. As she walked on, she felt thirst, so malevolent, so overpowering that she knelt on the sandy dunes.

Maybe the time is near, she reminded herself as she continued walking.

***

Her brother had questioned her till dusk, hoping to get the names of the perpetrators. She did not budge. She insisted that she doesn't remember anything. Her maids informed her that her brother had sworn revenge. He called upon numerous physicians to attend to her, to restore her mutilated self, but in vain.

She saw Janaki one day then, guarded by the fiercest warriors of Lanka.

And she knew it was the end.

***

The ocean waves crashed against each other foaming and frothing. She put down her rucksack and sucked in her breath. She stood by the shore, thinking of how the world had forgotten the tale of the benevolent and mighty Lankapati, replacing it with a ten-headed demon who coveted another man's wife and led himself to his doom.

She was no longer known as Chandranakha or Meenakshi, as lovingly called by her mother.

She is going to be remembered as Shurpanakha, the demoness whose lust drove an entire kingdom to its ruin.

As she resumed walking, she felt, there would be a day, aeons later, when the world shall know her tale.

A wave crashed against the abandoned rucksack, devouring it.

11

MANDARA

by Rukma Anil

Y ou wretched woman!"

The screams echoed through the courtyard as Kaikeyi ran along the corridor. She hurriedly lifted me. I stood up half my height, bent and humiliated. Bharatha helped me on the stick. I would play this memory until the day I died. It was Sumitra's son. Shatrughna.

"I wish you rot in hell". Shatrughna muttered under his breath as he left.

Way past my prime, in greying finery, humped on my back, I felt the pathetic little gazes swarm me. From the maids, the page boys, Kaikeyi and Bharatha.

"Let me help you to your room, mother". It was Bharatha. The kind, sweet one. As mother and son escorted me to my old room, I heard the chambermaids think," Serves her right. If it weren't for her, we would have had our crown prince in the palace. He would have been King". Kaikeyi served a glass of water as Bharata eased me onto the mattress. She sat by my side. Bharatha took leave.

I observed Kaikeyi. She had aged years after that day's incident. I could read her. I knew her well. I was her governess. Well, some say we were sisters even. Some used to call me Rekha. Until they did not. I was a princess too, in a former life. I remember the endless number of suitors who asked for my hand. Even before Kaikeyi was born. I took good care of myself. I adorned myself with the prettiest garlands of jasmine and champak. To be a woman was to be bewitchingly beautiful. I had to preserve that gift. So, I treated my body to the best of perfumes, and cleansers like red sandalwood.

I remember the day when Kaikeyi was born. She was entrusted to me. She was beautiful, just like me. With her wide eyes and a black tuft of hair. I loved her. She was my own.

Her eyes were not that wide or curious now. I couldn't recognise if those were her eyelids or just layers of sadness and guilt drooping over those pretty eyes. She was angry. I could tell that. She would not look at me. She wouldn't speak to me. I think it was more convenient this way. As I drank the water, I thought of the days we spent running around the palace grounds. Trying to get Kaikeyi to eat.   I taught her everything I knew. Arts, Music, Governance, Literature. I watched her change. She was six. She would try to walk like me. With her juvenile attempts of bending her hips at angles in an awkward gait and I would laugh and tell her "That's not how I walk and then sway my hips and turn around and say "See, that's how you do it".

It all started with a dull ache in the back. Every morning when I woke up. With every passing day, I felt my sight go deeper into the ground. Until one day I couldn't see more than a man who looked at me and steered away. He was a messenger from a kingdom. Father looked dejected. No one wanted to marry me. And that day I knew I could not lift my neck up. I had to crane it sideways to not feel the crippling pain that I felt. No herbs could help me. No vapours or massage could straighten the spine. Nothing excited me. The perfumes, garlands and the cleansers reminded me of Rekha. So did Kaikeyi as she swayed her hips when she walked. With years, my skin became dark and it wrinkled. My palms crackled like parchment. I became Mandara the hunchback, the maid of Kaikeyi.

However, there was one part of my beauty that flourished. It grew into a warrior, wrapped itself in fierceness and swayed its hips as it walked. It was Kaikeyi. As for me, I draped myself in drab colours. I watched Kaikeyi as she got married to Dasharatha. I bore witness to her yielding Bharatha. I was there in Ayodhya throughout the boys' childhood. I was provided for. Food, fine clothes, fragrant rooms, you name it. Sumitra and Kausalya treated me like their mother. I was almost their age. They would leave me out of their conversations out of respect for my 'age'. I wondered if, by age, they meant my ugliness. With Kaikeyi being the youngest wife and Dasharatha's favourite, we grew apart. We would greet each other in the corridors, or she would send for me if she needed me. Being Mandara was difficult. I had no form or purpose. I had no place in the court or the palace. Who was I? A wife? A mother? A courtier? A concubine? Nothing. I, Mandara, did not have a home. What troubled me the most probably was Kaikeyi. She had all that I wished for. To love her was to love my past. To hate her was to hate myself. I would like to tell myself that I loved Kaikeyi dearly that I could not bring Mandara to be happy. The distance was suffocating.

The boys loved playing. I was trying to stroll through the gardens with its green leaves and lush foliage. Rama, the eldest one had thrown a ball. It landed near my foot. I bend down to pick it up. As I flung it in the air, it fell away from him. He was angry. He was a child. It must have hurt him that he missed the shot. As for me, I couldn't move much. He came running to me. Poor boy must have felt sad. As I tried to reach him, he struck me with his bat and ran into the palace crying in anger. I picked myself up. As I walked to my room to change, I heard Kausalya "No Rama. She is not ugly. She is just old and tired." Rama had called me ugly. He was a child. And he felt I was ugly.

As I retired to my room, I saw Bharatha run up to me. "Mandara mother," the voice called. "Does it hurt? I am sorry. Rama did not want to hurt you. The Bat only flew" I looked at him. His eyes shone like little stars. He had Kaikeyi's eyes. Propping myself on a cushion, I motioned Bharatha towards me and said, "You will come across Mandaras. They can be ugly. Please promise me you won't hurt them. Word or deed.". Bharatha looked at me and said "I won't hurt Mandaras. You are not ugly. I like you." Bharatha ran away as he said this. I watched him run out through the curtains. I felt he was a kind, sweet boy.

The years turned in. Dasharatha had sent the boys to study under sage Vashishta, a few years back. I heard the eldest one had managed to secure himself King Janaka's daughter, Janaki. They say she is very beautiful. That she was the daughter of the earth. That Janaka found her in a box when he inaugurated the ploughing of the land that year. I feel bad for whoever had to put that girl in a box. As for Bharatha, he married Kushadwaja's daughter, Mandavi. I can't wait to see him with his wife.

"The princes and their consorts are arriving. They are at the gates"

I dragged myself enthusiastically to greet my Bharatha. Kaikeyi's Bharatha. As I neared, I saw Kaikeyi excitedly embracing a boy. It was the eldest one. Disgusting!!! Why would Kaikeyi receive Rama so enthusiastically while Bharatha stood beside him? She fed Rama sweets and then fed Bharatha. She always had a soft spot for Rama. He is not even her own child. How could she love both of them the same? Why does everyone love Rama so much? Why is he everybody's favourite? I had greater plans for Kaikeyi. For us. Why did she have so much love for Kausalya's son?

A messenger had later informed me that, Dasharatha, was planning to choose the heir to the kingdom. I was getting old. The princes were of age. Kaikeyi glowed like the befitting sun of the Ikshvakus. It was unsettling. Dasharatha nominating an heir would mean one of the boys would become king. Where does that place his mother? The Queen Mother. Now, if Rama were to be king that would mean less power for Kaikeyi. Where would that place me? The hunchback maid of Kaikeyi?

As soon as word reached me, that Rama was chosen to be king. I wanted to have an audience with Kaikeyi. I met her in her chambers. The huge mirror, with an assortment of aromatic cosmetics and balms at the corner of the room. There she was. Retiring for the day. Taking off the rubies from her ears. Rama will be king in 2 days. I decided to set this right. For me.

"So, Rama will be king."

"He will make a good king."

She pulled out a pearl garland and handed them to me with a smile. I saw a flicker of hurt through the smile. I saw the heaviness in her smile. Kaikeyi was very happy for Rama. But she also felt sad that Bharatha was not even considered. Dasharatha had revelled about how happy Kaikeyi was about Rama becoming the King. He did not know her as well as Mandara.

"But is good often enough?"

"My son is the loyal brother of the King."

"But he is not the King. What does that make you?"

She looked at me like the ground beneath her feet had slipped.

"Rama is as much a son to me as he is to Kausalya."

"That he is. But you are not Kausalya. We do not know what kind of a king Rama would make. But Bharatha is your son. He is kind and fair and loyal. If Bharatha becomes the king, you become the Queen mother." People will talk, Kaikeyi, that your son did not deserve to be a ruler. While in your heart you know, Bharatha would have made an excellent ruler. Will you be able to live with the guilt of not having fought for your son? For something you very well know, he deserves?"

"Think about it."

"It's too late. Mandara."

"Not yet. You have something from the war. Two, actually."

The next thing was the coronation. Kaikeyi claimed her boons. Rama left for Vanavasa. Bharatha became king. Dasharatha headed heavenwards. Urmila slept for 14 years. Lakshman accompanied Rama and Janaki. Rama would ask Janaki to take the Agnipariksha to prove her chastity. Deep in my heart, I always knew, Rama was insecure about his dark skin, Janaki's beauty, and virtue. A poor little boy. He never grew out of it. The rest is history.

Not a day passed without Kaikeyi regretting that day. Bharatha still rules in Rama's stead.

"Mandara" I lost track. It was Kaikeyi. "Let me know if you need anything".

As she walked out, she stopped at the entrance. She turned to look at me. The look hinted disgust for me. I would not blame her. It was a moment of weakness. She had given in. And to think I made it happen gives me a sense of relief. The world doesn't remember Mandaras. We are insignificant. We don't have bodies to speak of in an age when Manu endorsed fair maidens. We are punished for the crimes we did not commit. Who can make this better for us? A good ruler. Who else could it be other than the little boy who did not think that Mandara was ugly?

12

SUPERMAN

by Sandhra Sunil

Was that my superman toy on that teak table? I walked up to it, grazed my fingers. 15 years ago, I was too old to make a fuss over this missing piece of hero. I had a greater mess to clean up; a mess made by a person who should have been my real-time hero. Instead, he had run away, too cowardly to face it. Just a week ago, when I received his mail, I had not known if I wanted to meet him. But I deserved answers, seeking which I stand here in his house today.

My phone vibrated; it was Daniel asking me if everything was okay. I smiled. Although we had dated through college, it took the death of my mom two months back for me to gain the courage to come out to the world as gay and to move in with Daniel. Why wait? For my mom, I was this perfect kid and ever since dad abandoned us, she only became more protective around me. I was morally obliged not to cause her any pain instantly and put it off to later.

But this love she had for me did not stop her from giving the love of her body to other men. Even when dad lived with us, my mom would let men into her chambers during the day, leaving me with my cartoons. She chose her lovers with finesse, for she was a rare blend of a passionately dignified woman who did what she did because she chose to. Despite all the blotches in her character that one could point out, my mother loved me. Only, she was too full of herself and always shuttling between her lovers and her job as a receptionist, leaving her with no ears to what I had to say. So, I grew up, walls and toys making do for human presence and companionship.

"Jagan…?" a voice came from behind.

I turned back. He looked different, my dad; fifteen years can do a lot indeed.

"You're all grown, my boy," Dad said, hugging me. Awkwardly I hugged back. Behind him, a man as old as dad walked in, greying hairline, dressed in a crisp blue shirt. "Meet Mr. Vivek, my business partner," he said, and the man shook hands with me with a gentle smile.

"Sit Jagan, sit, sit, please…. God, how long… what shall I get you? Black tea? No don't look surprised, I follow you on Facebook, I know a lot you see…" he tattled.

"I am here for answers if you will excuse me… You mailed that you'd explain everything and I'm here because I wanted them. That's all that is there to this meeting," I said firmly.

Why did I hate him, you ask? Well, what man lets other men have his woman? He knew, I was sure, of my mother's quest for love but never confronted her. He never spoke at home, not even to mom, never attended my PTA meetings and never put me to sleep. He did get me loads of toys and my favourite chocolates but otherwise pretended like mom and I never existed. I wished he had taught me to ride the bicycle and let me scrape my knee now and then. When other boys made essays and speeches on their parents, I scripted my sweet hopes. Somewhere along my teens, I used to envy my friends for having constant fights and encountering endless lectures from their father. I longingly looked at my neighbour teaching his son to shave. I craved for a father who would have noticed my sexuality right during my adolescence. I did not think I hated him until he deserted us. I even blame him for my mother's affairs. In short, I hold him responsible for ruining the memories I should have had of a happy family because of his indifference.

My father stopped his sentence midway with my outburst and smiled faintly.

"Jagan, I was only 22 when I married Priyanka. My family was in the throes of suicide; my father had died of heart failure after his business ran aground. Priyanka's father showed us a light at the end of the tunnel- he offered to help me start a business provided I married Priyanka. Why choose a man from a crumbling family for his precious daughter? Because Priyanka, just 18 then, had eloped with a boy only to return three days later, after the boy had had enough of her. To make a 'good woman' of her, the condition of my family seemed really opportune to her father. So, there I found myself, for the sake of keeping my family alive, marrying a woman who did not care to look at me twice. My life changed; I started a business with her father's help. You could ask me why I ran away after 10 years of marriage. Why not run away earlier? I had two younger sisters and to marry them off, I had to stay.

And you... born of a loveless union, why cause you misery? Believe me when I say I did not want to add another person merely to suffer. But Priyanka was an unabashed person who sought her pleasures in men outside our marriage. And what right had I over a woman who was as uninterested in the marriage as I was? Nevertheless, she wanted a baby; a baby from her legal husband. Strange as it may sound, this coming from a woman who had illicit affairs meant only one thing- she knew that her lovers would never take responsibility for a child. So I gave in, and we had you. As much as I did not wish for a child under such circumstances, I loved you with all my heart. Remember your youngest aunt's wedding... you were such an adorable boy in your little suit..."

Of course, how could I forget? The last time I saw my dad was at that wedding. He held me in his hand for a long time that night. That was the last anyone in our family saw of him and the beginning of my hatred for a deserter. Until today; today I had answers.

"But why leave us? If you loved me so much, could you not have stayed in the marriage just for my sake? Millions of women do it every day; my mother did it all her life. Was I not a reason good enough to stay? Why run away? You're just trying to justify your desertion!" I raised my voice, tears in my eyes. The man was at the verge of making me forgive him, but I was not giving in. I hated him then, I hate him now and I shall hate him forever.

He smiled gently again.

"Do you see that superman? That toy of yours? I've held on to that for years now. When I migrated to this place, all that kept me alive was that toy and the thoughts of you. You were my strength, son, and my reason for existence even though it was away from you. And as to why I ran away..."

He gently smiled at Mr. Vivek who was seated next to him, took his hand, and entwined their fingers. And there I found two rings shining.

"I hope you understand Jagan... because right now, only you will..."

13

A DISH WELL SERVED

by Sanjana Varma

GRAHAM

I have seen your work. I am willing to set you up for life if you are willing to work for me," the Cigarette Ad voice said through the phone.

"I don't know what you are talking about," replied Graham, stumped.

"That girl on Figaro Street, the one with the bashed -head. You did it, didn't you? I have been keeping tabs on you," the voice sneered.

"You got it all wrong. Just leave me alone."

Graham disconnected and threw away the phone. His hands were trembling. They knew!

He heard the whisper in his ear again. That girl with the bashed head and swollen lips was crawling towards him. In a raspy voice, she said, "You did this to me. Look at me! Look what you did to me!"

He moved back crying. NO, no. She was in front of him, blooding oozed from her head! A guttural sound escaped from her throat. He summoned his strength, took the remote from the bed and threw it on her. He was alone.

He quickly rushed to the washroom. The water felt extra cold on his hands. He washed his face muttering, "Wake up, wake up. You are dreaming. She is dead. You made sure of that."

He cast a look in the mirror. His face was pale, lack of sleep apparent under the eyes. His phone beeped making him jump out of his skin.

Call me when you change your mind.

He turned on the news. She was all over the news.

"Jane Doe of Figaro Street remains aloof from justice. Her killer seems a pro and has left no clue. The Police say they don't have anything to go on. Four months have passed and now sadly, she will remain nameless forever."

He sighed in relief. They didn't know. But what about the man who called? One job he said. He gazed outside; the storm clouds stood in a battalion ready for the war. He dialled the unknown number.

***

ASTER

The café was bustling as usual. Commuters came in to have a cup of tea before heading home. Teenagers were their loud selves. The old gentleman was in his corner, sipping tea and reading the paper. Aster was having a good day. Her customers were happy, the business was buzzing. Angus hummed a little tune while he worked. The 80's music, her favourite played in the background. Not too loud to interfere with the chatter, but just right like the amount of salt in her food. She took orders from the couple on the left and went to prepare it.

"Burger and fries for Table 7," shouted a busboy.

"Coming right up!" chimed Angus.

Aster started on the burger when her eyes fell on the news.

Poor girl! That's a bloody way to die. The Police gave up. Gives me the shudders when I think of it," said Teres behind her.

"I know," she replied.

The busboy picked up the order and left.

She was about to ask Teres something when her phone rang. 'Mom' announced the phone. She quickly picked up the call.

"Are you safe?"

"Mom, what's wrong? Ya, I am fine."

"That girl on the news, dear! She's your age, I can't help worrying. You are alone in the city."

"I am ok Mom. She used to live in a different part of town."

"Be careful and call me after work."

"Will do, and don't overthink."

She disconnected the call and watched the people. She always knew that everyone has their demons. Some sin to wrestle with and perhaps overcome. This was the best part of the day, she felt like a detective who uncovers the secrets behind the faces. Her eyes were attuned to the slight change of emotions on the myriad faces. With an imagination so wild she cooked up stories to amuse herself. Anyone could be the killer, all seemingly normal yet hiding something sinister underneath! She thought of the poor girl. It could be me, it could be anyone I know. The realization sent a shiver down her spine. She shrugged off the dark thoughts. Fixed her best smile and went to greet the new patrons.

***

GRAHAM

He took deep breaths and hit the call button.

"I knew you would call. You made the right decision," the man said.

"How do you know I did it? How can I trust you?"

"Graham, I am a man with a need. I have my ways. I saw you doing it. Your secret is safe with me. I am your ally."

"What do I get?"

"A million and a new identity. Do the deed and you will have a new lease on life."

"Who?"

"You will receive a package with the details. Follow the instructions."

"Who are you?"

"Just a poor-rich gentleman in need of a favour. You can call me Nigel Goodman."

"Nigel Goodman, you have my word."

"I'll call you."

The line went dead. He googled Nigel Goodman. The head of the Goodman Empire, filthy rich with a taste for blonde women. A man in his 50s with the physique of a runner.

"Fine. I'll bite," he whispered to himself and poured a glass of rum.

Graham woke up to the ring of his phone. It's Goodman again.

"Graham, your package is at your front door. It has all the details you need to know about the pest that needs to be put down."

"I need money."

"It's there. Be very careful. This girl is on to me, to tear down my family. I want her dead."

"I will take care."

Graham opened the blinds, shielding his eyes from the sunlight. The clock said 3 pm. He got up and opened the door of his single-room apartment. A brown package awaited him. He took it, throwing glances around to make sure no one was there. The door thud shut. He tore the package open. Inside was a file with pictures and details. An envelope containing wads of 500 slipped out. He couldn't believe his luck. He opened the file. A beautiful dark-haired girl in her 20s met his eyes. Aster was her name. It seemed that Aster wanted Nigel to accept her as his illegitimate daughter. She claimed he had ditched his mother for the blonde on his arm now. Graham's lips twisted into a sneer. He got up, took a long shower, planning his move. This would be his last work as Graham. He wanted to relish it, every ounce of it.

***

ASTER

She loved the café as if it's her own baby. She looked at all the happy faces. Wooden- tables with chairs around, the big bookshelf on the corner, the warmth of the kitchen on the opposite side. Hanging lights dispelled the gloom that managed to sneak in during the rain. Busboys were energetic and the chef was amazing, she has been getting compliments from the customers. How she adored them! The patrons love it when she comes around to make sure they are comfortable. She prided over that fact. Aster could vouch anywhere that she knew all her patrons.

A man got inside just then. He was around 6 ft, wearing washed-out jeans and black tee. There was a cap on his head backwards. "I haven't seen this one before," she thought. There was an air of gloom about him.

"Hey! What can I get you?" she asked with a warm smile.

"I'll have a BLT and a beer. Thanks," came the clipped response.

"Right! Are you new here?"

"Ya, I haven't come here before."

She nodded and turned away. He was good looking, tanned skin and dark hair. There was something that drew her towards him, an attraction of sorts. She couldn't place a finger on it.

Her phone beeped with a text. She ignored it and went to get the order. She watched that man, lost in his own world. He wasn't waiting for anyone. He sat there taking his time. Aster went on with her chores. An hour later, she saw him getting up. He gave her a quick shy glance which made the colour rise in her cheeks.

Around 9, she cleaned the place and locked the café. She needs to be quick to catch the 9:15 metro. Aster walked fast into the station. 9: 10 she glanced at her watch. Thank God.

A familiar voice greeted her.

"Hey! I came to the café on the 7th."

"Hey! Ya, I remember."

"Nice place you have there, and great food"

"Thanks. Glad you liked it"

Aster knew what was coming.

"Can I have your number if it is ok with you?"

Aster suppressed a smile and gave her card.

"Cool! Maybe we can meet somewhere. I don't have many friends. My name is Greg by the way."

"Sounds cool!"

The metro glided on to the platform. Aster got in and waved to him. He smiled and waved.

"What were you even thinking? For all you know he could be a killer or a flirt. You just gave him your number! What if he is a creep?" Her mind drove her into a panic mood. She could imagine Teres having a laugh when she tells about it.

***

GRAHAM

Target Acquired

He sent a text to Goodman.

He sat down on the old couch and plotted his next move.

Hey, it's Greg. I hope you reached home safe.

Hey, ya. That's sweet of you.

Can we meet this Saturday?

Ya, sure. I'll text you the details.

Cool

He will ask her out and get it done!

Nigel called.

"I got your text. I want to be there when you end her. You got me? I want to see it for myself."

"I hear you. What should I do?"

"Lure her to the Blind Street off of 7th. There is an old shop. I will wait for you there. Before you go to meet her, meet me first."

"Why?"

"Let's settle our deal. You kill her and you are free to go. I will pay you before. I don't want any risks. We won't meet again."

"As long as I get my money"

"8 pm Saturday then."

"Bye"

Must be some sadistic nut! To see your own Blood die. Rich people and their whims! Bah! Graham thought.

***

ASTER

Aster's heart was all aflutter. This is it! It's been a while since she had some fun. She couldn't wait for Saturday.

"I am going on a date"! She said.

Teres rolled her eyes! "So dreamy, '' she deadpanned.

"Shut up! I need a dress."

"You could wear that expensive dress your Dad gave you."

"Placating gift from my dear Dad? I could."

"There you go problem solved." She said rolling to the side on her bed and covering her head with the duvet.

Aster laughed. She changed and turned off the lights and hit the sack. Tomorrow is a new day.

***

SATURDAY

ASTER

The rush hour was on when she got a call.

"Hey, Greg! I was about to call you. Meet me at Steven's at 9?"

"Sounds great! I'll see you then!"

It was good. She had something to look forward to. She had packed the dress in her bag. It is going to be a good night!

***

GRAHAM

He packed a small bag, only essentials ready for the getaway! He cast one long glance at his home of 4 years. He took the glass of wine and toasted to himself in the mirror.

"To a new life! Goodbye Graham. Welcome Fred!" he chuckled to himself.

7: 30 on the dot, he got out of his apartment. The old shop was deserted like the street where the cab dropped.

The door was ajar. Nigel might be there. He made way into the shop. It was dark. He turned on the flashlight of the phone.

"Goodman, I am here," he shouted.

He sensed a movement to the side.

"Hello, are you there?" Graham glanced at his phone to see if there is any text from him when he felt a hard smack behind his head.

When he came to his senses, he was on a chair. His head hurt and his arms too. He opened his eyes to a room filled with light. He couldn't move his arms. He saw that he was getting drugged. He was drowsy and out of strength.

His eyes adjusted to the light. Slowly, he saw a figure stepping out from the shadows.

Aster stepped forward! Relief flooded him.

"You are here! I am so glad to see you. Please save me!"

"You are asking the wrong person Graham!" she said with a smirk.

"How... Who are you?"

She took her phone and played a recorded audio, Cigarette Ad voice of Nigel Goodman.

"You, it was all you! Why?"

"For the girl you killed. I was there Graham, I saw you." She walked around not taking her eyes off him.

"How many times did she ask to let her go? I was scared. You would have killed me too."

Graham laughed, "We are the same. You have the taste for blood. " Hoping to turn the odds in his way.

"I have the taste for blood but unlike her you deserve it. You see, I didn't lie. You will get a new identity. That's Flakka you are on. Say goodbye to yourself, you will pay for what you did!"

" No, please! I didn't have a choice. She was screaming."

"You had a choice. You could have let her live. But, no, you were so drunk! So full of being the one in power! You live for that power over someone. The ecstasy of it, to feel the life drain from them while you watch! You won't get another chance!"

Aster bends to set the leg of the chair on fire. "Goodbye, Graham," she said with a glint of satisfaction.

"No, please. Let me go!"

She stood aside, watching the flames lick him up. Each sear made him scream until it was heard no more. She took the note from her pocket. Left it on the floor once the flame died and left.

Teres woke her up the next morning," Aster, check out the news, Jane Doe's killer was found dead."

They turned on the news. The Investigator said, "This man was found to have taken his own life. We got a note next to him in which he claims he was the killer. Officers have discovered the murder weapon from his place. Finally, she can rest."

Aster smiled. Yes, finally she can rest.

14

LITTLE BROTHER

by J. Jerome

Questions?" Davis asked and paused. His piercing green eyes scanned the people inside the room. He then nodded his head slowly after a moment of silence and the collective stillness of the determined, young eyes that stared back at him. "You all know what to do. Get out there and give 'em hell!" he exclaimed as his battle-hardened face turned into a twisted mass of skin, determination, and adrenaline. The young officers before him saluted as one and stomped on the grey concrete floor with such vigour and pride. They had the untampered fire of youth and a dangerous objective to match it.

It was exactly what every glory-seeking young officer was looking for.

***

"This is it, guys. Three key objectives, three handsome commanders to accomplish it," Oliver said proudly with an arrogant look on his face.

"Speak for yourselves," Lizzie replied immediately. She rolled her eyes as she shook her head at her two male companions. "There is such a thing as a handsome woman, sweetheart," Oliver explained, slightly embarrassed. "Don't just smile there, Julien.

Help me out!" he added as he turned to Julien who worked on the lace of his boots.

"You got yourself in this trouble, Oliver. You have to get yourself out of it," Julien replied playfully as he shook his head.

"Aren't you supposed to be the expert at getting people out of prisons?" Oliver countered.

"Yes. And you are the master of bombs," Julien explained slowly. "So, you bombed it again with your girlfriend. As usual," he added with a grin.

"Very well said, Julien," Lizzie interjected then crossed her arms as she stared angrily at Oliver.

"Okay. Okay. My mistake. I take it back," Oliver said as he raised both of his arms as if surrendering.

"Good," Lizzie said triumphantly.

"But seriously, take care of yourselves out there. Get caught, but don't get killed. I wouldn't be able to get you out if you're dead. Understand?" Julien reminded his two best friends.

"Don't worry about me. I'll be hitting that senate douchebag from a mile away. I'll be out of there before they know where I was," Lizzie said softly as she gripped Julien's shoulder tightly.

"Same here," Oliver said as he nodded to Julien. "I'm bombing that weapons development site and everyone in it. They'd all be ash before they know what hit them," he added as he slapped Julien's shoulder.

Julien nodded slowly at both of them and then watched them kiss each other on the lips the way only two people who are deeply in love could kiss. Julien stomped his boots on the floor and tightened the straps of his equipment.

"We're ready to go, Commander!" an eager voice interrupted the two lovers kissing.

"I'll be right there," Oliver replied in a slightly irritated tone. Winston saluted and left the locker room in silence.

"I swear, I'm just about to make a manual bomb and have Winston detonate it on site," Oliver whispered to his two friends.

"You can't. You're their commander. It's your duty to take care of them," Julien explained patiently.

"He always interrupts my time with Lizzie!" Oliver replied angrily.

"That's not a good reason to get one of your men killed," Lizzie added with a sigh.

"Fine. I'll just get him transferred, then."

***

Six groups went out at the same time. The first three had the task of creating separate distractions across the city; a bank robbery, a major fire at a commercial area, and several bomb threats.

The distractions across the city had barely gone off when the security detail of Senator Derrick Bradley decided to make a last-minute change to their security plans—move him out of his hotel and take him outside the city to his summer home.

They reacted faster than the plan had anticipated.

Fortunately, Lizzie had a habit of getting into position earlier than planned as well. She was ready to take the shot as soon as she noticed the sudden security movement inside the senator's hotel.

***

A black van screeched to a halt in front of the eastern gate of the secret rebel base. The people in the vicinity all jumped to their feet and approached the black van with a hand on the pistol on their chest.

All except for Lizzie who approached the van confidently while her face was masked with the look of worry and concern.

"Stay clear! Make way!" A man in black overall and a red armband shouted as soon as he jumped out of the van. He ran to the back of the van and opened the door with Lizzie closely behind him.

"What happened?" Lizzie asked softly. Her voice was almost breaking.

"He got shot pulling one of his men out. He's stable but still unconscious," the medic reported.

Lizzie felt her heart breaking and yet relieved at the same time as she watched them rush the unconscious Julien into the base.

***

The beeping of machinery brought his mind back to consciousness as he slowly became aware of his surroundings. He kept his eyes closed and allowed his other senses to get as much information as they could without giving any hint that he's already awake. He remembered getting shot as they were escaping. And he lost consciousness just as he reached one of the escape vehicles. He wondered if he was captured. He never planned on getting captured.

However, before he could do anything, his nose caught the faint scent of magnolia. His body reacted immediately to the smell and he noticed his heartbeat run faster. He had to force himself not to smile as he slowly opened his eyes.

"You're finally awake!" Lizzie exclaimed and punched Julien in the gut.

"Ow! I just got shot there!" he complained loudly.

"Well, that's for not being careful!" Lizzie replied back. Her face looked grim behind a bittersweet smile.

"You're so mean! I should complain to Oliver instead!" Julien said as he struggled to sit up. Lizzie helped him up and he immediately noticed the tears that edged in her lovely almond-shaped eyes.

"Where's that big oaf, anyway?" Julien asked with a tone of worry.

"He-Umm... They... They did not survive," Lizzie replied slowly as she choked on her words, fighting back the tears as if the world would end if she failed.

"What do you mean? Did they get caught? Help me out of here and I'll get him back here!" Julien exclaimed angrily. His face turned red as his lips quivered.

"There's no getting him back, Jule. He was badly injured. They tried to save him, but he did not survive," Lizzie explained with a brave voice that sounded like a stretched Japanese paper getting battered by the wind that she kept clearing her throat in between the words. "He had seven gunshot wounds. Everyone on his squad either died on the operating table or died on the field. No one survived," she confessed with a deep sigh that sounded like she had just breathed her last.

"I'm sorry Lizzie. I don't know what to say. He always seems unbreakable. I never imagined that he would ever fall during a mission," Julien said slowly.

"I suppose no one is really unbreakable," Lizzie replied.

"No." It was all that Julien was able to say. He held back everything that he wanted to say in his mind and allowed Lizzie to have a quiet time to grieve.

"We've both lost a lot to the rebellion," Lizzie said softly. "You lost your sister. I lost Oliver. I wonder what our lives would've been like if we didn't get mistaken for rebels when we were in college almost six years ago," she continued.

"They would both still be alive now, I'm sure," he replied as he stared at the floor with teary eyes. "I should've done more to keep everyone safe. My sister was all I had, and I failed her," he complained. "Now, I have failed Oliver too," he said as his voice trailed off.

Lizzie reached out her hand and held Julien's hand tightly. "What happened to Oliver was not your fault. No one could have known that they would fail," she said in a soft voice. She wanted to comfort him and tell him that everything would be okay; that they still have each other, but the pain of losing Oliver forced her to hide behind the suffering in her heart.

"But I could have been there! I could have helped with the bombing before I went to rescue the Vice Leader. I could've done something!"

"There was nothing that you could have done. If you helped him before freeing the Vice Leader, they would have fortified the prison before you got there, and we would've lost you and failed to get the Vice Leader."

"But you don't know that."

"Yeah, I do. We all stuck to the plan and you got shot. That would've been worse if the two of you didn't go with the plan."

Julien was about to say something, but Lizzie gripped his hand even tighter and he decided to stay quiet. The faint smell of magnolias and her hand on his hand calmed him down as his head spun around at her scent.

"All we have is each other now," Julien whispered. His voice was so soft that it was easy to miss what he said, but all of her senses were tuned in to him at that moment.

"Yes. All we have now is each other and the rebellion."

"Each other and the rebellion," he echoed.

"You have to stop risking your life. You can't save the world on your own."

"Shouldn't we at least try?"

"But you've already done so much! You saved us when we were mistaken as rebel spies when we were in college. I'm alive right now because of you."

"I feel like I should do more!"

"No. I can't lose a brother too."

"Am I the older brother that you never had?"

"More like the younger brother who never listens to me," Lizzie replied with a slight grin. A tear suddenly streaked down her cheek as she let her guard down for a split second. She took a deep breath and stood up from the bed. "I better let you rest; you lost a lot of blood."

"Where are you going?"

"I'll report to the High Leader that you're awake. Talk to you later Jule," Lizzie said as she exited the door to Julien's room. He stared at her as she slowly closed the door and kept staring at the door long after she's gone.

'She sees me as a brother only?' Julien thought to himself. His face remained expressionless as his right hand gripped the edge of the bed tightly.

***

"Exactly a week ago, I was rescued from incarceration by the team led by Commander Julien Marks. And because of their success, we now approach the final stage of our ultimate goal," Timothy paused and turned towards the direction of Julien and Lizzie. He nodded his head at them and then turned towards the crowd in front of him once more. "As you all know, I was captured by the military more than four months ago," he continued. "What most of you do not know is that getting caught was part of the plan. I had to get into the prison and talk to the only person who knows about a secret entrance into the palace."

There was a murmur in the crowd that quickly rose into a crescendo. It was quickly muted when Timothy raised his hand. A proud smile found its way to his lips.

"And I was able to get the information that we need to get into the palace and strike a fatal blow on the government." The underground auditorium was filled with a thunderous roar. The rebels all raised a clenched fist into the air. "Unfortunately, our asset inside did not survive long after I received the information," he continued with a sad tone. "Old age got to him. As it will get to all of us. But not before we topple this government of lies!" Another thunderous roar filled the chamber. Only Julien and Lizzie were not screaming out their lungs like the rest. There was a smile on Lizzie's face while Julien's face remained an emotionless mask.

"Are you okay?" Lizzie asked Julien when she noticed his expressionless face.

"I'm okay and overjoyed. But I can't get over-excited or risk bursting my stitches."

"Right."

Timothy raised both his hands and the crowd grew quiet once more. "We'll call back all the cells and start preparing for the final battle that will bring the government to its final bloody hour!" the chamber shook with the screams and stomping of the rebels who heard the declaration of the Vice Leader. Davis, the High Leader stood by the side of his brother and clapped his hands.

"It's finally about to end, Jule."

"Yes. It's all about to end."

"Have you thought about what you'd do once we've established a new government?"

"Of course," Julien replied as he stared straight at Lizzie.

***

Just as Julien expected, he'd be the first to be sent out to scout the secret entrance to the palace. He was the expert in getting people out, it only made sense that he was the only choice for this.

The entrance was inside an old service tunnel that was not properly sealed off after the construction of the subway was complete. The contractor obviously cut corners, and no one knew about it except the engineer who was in charge of sealing it.

Based on the information, sewage access should lead him right under one of the palace's storm drains near the kitchen. He searched around the weak cavern walls and eventually found the one that leads to the sewer system of the palace. It was not long before he finally found the one that led directly to the western side of the kitchen.

He climbed up and silently opened the drain cover. He almost jumped off the ladder when he heard a familiar voice.

"Silent as a mouse, as always Colonel Marks. We have been waiting for you," the voice said as a muscular hand extended in front of Julien to help him up. He grabbed the hand and got up from the tunnel.

"General Higgins. Nice of you to welcome me personally."

"In truth, I was just taking a cigarette break when you arrived. Any news for me colonel?"

"They called back all the rebel cells. The time to crush the rebellion has come. They'd be well-armed, but they're overcrowded inside that base which is an advantage for the military."

"That's great news! Good job!"

"Timothy getting caught was a setup. They knew that the engineer who knew about this secret entrance was in that prison."

"That's a plan that we didn't anticipate. Any tips for other surprises like that?"

"Yes. Kill everyone but capture their prime assassin at all costs. She knows about missions and people that only Timothy or Davis knows about, but she doesn't have their charisma to rebuild the rebellion. So, she's safe for capture and interrogation."

"What's her name again?"

"Lizzie. Lizzie Eliot."

15

BILLET DOUX

by Ruchka Gulati

A swivel mirror catches a glimpse as she knots a chignon with embellished pins holding it at the slender nape of her neck. Maya lifts the phial of perfume, then dabs a dot behind each ear, one on the collar bones and one each on each pulse points on wrists, and as if to catch the waft drags her wrist to her face, inhaling deeply the tantalising smell of Orris and Bergamot. A well-practised final step to allure. A smile adorns her face as she sets forth on a path traversed every night. A midnight maidens quest to quench her revenge. A facade hides her inner turmoil ravaged with deceit.

She puts the ring on her finger, twirls it and a glaze comes before her eyes. The beatific smile gets replaced by a throttled anguish of pain.

Memories stoked, of the day when she stumbled on sealed envelopes of letters tied with a red ribbon of illicit liaison.

It was a cold winter morning, the sun's bleak rays filtered through the sheer. She awoke with a start as the pillow next to her was plump and his side of the bedsheet creaseless and vacant. The first sign of fear engulfed her as she pressed the cell to call him. No response. No communication was poor communication in her definition of rules of love and matrimony. She furiously checked for missed calls or messages. None. Trepidation now sought a home in her mind. Maybe an accident or maybe in a drunken stupor he was lying outside a bar. Robert was a compulsive drinker. He hit the bar each day, came home in an inebriated state. Then the morning light saw a different man loving, caring and always attentive. Humane flaws matched in some ways.

She was a woman who gave too much and suffered from low self-esteem. For her, she deserved no better. Robert was handsome, had all that makes a good husband, a condo and car with money to lavish her with a lifestyle most women would desire and seek. His drinking was an anomaly she ignored, survived, and existed with. For there was much else that overtook her emotions. Having lived a life of abandonment this was bliss.

Maya moved into the kitchen and filled the kettle for a morning cuppa of her favourite elixir- coffee. Most needed now to get her brain cells in action mode. When a sudden thought struck her to check his closet for his rolodex and dial a friend or business partner. Maybe he had to make an urgent trip out of the city and is still in flight she mulled. Rummaging through his armoury with the coffee mug in one hand Maya sighted something that caught her eye.

A rosewood casket lay beneath a pile of woollens. Well hidden. Curiosity caught her as she has never seen this before. She was scared often to irk his ire so never questioned him much. Also except for his drinking habit, he had never given her reasons to doubt. Maya carefully without disturbing the contents around it tentatively brought it out and placed it in the glaring light of the sun on the centre table.

She could not help admiring the beauty of the box. It was exquisitely carved. Encased. Semi-precious stones were inlaid in gold filigree work. She carefully opened the clasp. It was lined on the inside with red velvet and on it lay a beautiful ring. A signet ring.

On the collet were gemstones and in the centre, glyptic words were plied- initials 'RC'. She lifted it in her hand and looked at it. Its inside rim was inscribed with the words 'Love, Cheryl'

Maya's heart took a lurch and with quivering hands, she examined stared dumbfounded. Rejecting all thoughts that came riding. From her remotest crannies came sounds of pain buried. A cry rose from her lips and she dropped it in the box as if it had burnt her fingers. Then with fumbling hands picked it up again. Looked at it once again with a cornucopia of mingled thoughts. She saw some glaring truths that signalled at an affair. It's difficult to imagine what thoughts raced through her mind as she tried to place it back in the little niche in the velvet lining. She struggled here and pressed it hard and something gave way. The burgundy velvet lined base of the box caved in to reveal a concealed compartment. A scent of lavender pervaded her senses.

A red ribbon peeped from under sheaves of paper- the aforementioned documents of deceit

Billet Doux- love letters from Cheryl to Robert.

She sat transfixed and stared at the bundle till it became a blur on her retina. Twenty-one envelopes lay sealed. All marked numbered and each had on its front. 'Passion, love and hope' written in an elegant skilled scrawl. She could not fathom how when and where. So many questions raked her mind and so many thoughts prevailed. All came clouding and she could not even rationalize her existence. So, her marriage was a farce. All this was a farce. Nothing held meaning. Not the gifts of love, the nights of passion or this beautiful house for that matter. Their home. No, not home her mind argued. Walls, vacant walls that spelt deceit. She saw their wedding photograph on the credenza. She picked it up and threw it into the dustbin. The shards of broken glass pieces pierced the picture and impaled her mind too. The letters still lay on the table and she made a drink and sat down to unravel the secrets.

Curiosity to know about the woman that had taken her peace. This was torture in the true sense, but she wanted it and needed it too.

There were letters beautifully handwritten and the sheets smelled of lavender. They were deckle-edged, each on ivory colour handmade paper and on the right-hand top corner they bore the initials 'RC' in gold. Still perfumed by the gentle fumes of Cheryl and Robert's love. She inhaled and cursed herself for doing that. Could she cut her breath off! Another cry ripped her. She tormented her mind and imagined much more. Robert reading each one with love ardour and passion. She sat and read and killed herself as she went through each one. Drank the glass to the last dreg. Poured another and another. Soon her tears dried, and she felt strangely numb. Maybe drained of all emotions.

That was the day when she crumbled like a shapeless heap on the floor. Copious tears streamed down her beautiful face. She was oblivious to the cold marble floor. She sat with her head in the crook of her arm. No sound penetrated, no words escaped her dry parched lips, she was benumbed. She did not hear the click of footsteps on the marble floor or the incessant ring of the cell. She was oblivion to all.

Robert came and saw the letters scattered on the floor and he got his answer. He turned heel and walked out after picking them. Packed his bag, gathered his belongings, the casket and letters and all memories. He walked out. Maya stayed abandoned again. Her worst fears answered.

Robert sat with all and pondered. He knew he was justified in his actions. He knew he had done no wrong as he owned his life to Cheryl as much as he owed it to Maya. He loved them both. Now we may discourse and argue. Can a man love two women at the same time with so much love and not feel an iota of guilt or regret? Robert felt none. Robert had a medical history which he could not deny. He was polyamorous. And he would get into compulsive relationships. Till one or the other partner discovered him. He did not recognise this. Much as he knew about it in a sketched way. He always felt right. Blame it on maladies of the mind. As in his eyes, he was giving love truly to both and taking care. Medically he would have been sympathised with but socially he invoked no such reactions.

Maya knew no better and in her eyes, he was a man she abhorred and In fact, this hate extended to all men. Strange as it was she let this build her into a woman who became the Maya that men craved but dare not love. No man can do justice to two women at the same time she justified. He must love me less to seek another.

Day turned to night. Maya stirred and like a lifeless creature, drained, struggled to her feet and saw this post-it on Robert's closet-scribbled in his scrawl were two words 'Good Bye'.

They say when questions are left unanswered we suffer more. Nothing is more painful than an emotion that is in no way returned.

Her partner's amorous dalliance left a trail of lesions that scarred her heart and spoiled her for another man. She abstained from love for love failed her.

She shrugs her shoulders as if to get rid of it and in measured steps of elegance, she drifts into the night. When love bemoans, revenge takes strange roots and hers was a story which seems to mollify that to her aching mind.

Maya is an epitome of beauty. Her alabaster skin is smooth and unblemished. A face that is strikingly beautiful, soft grey eyes, bow-shaped lips and high cheekbones. Her long hair poker straight is a lovely caramel brown with lighter streaks that catch the sun rays and reflect. No wonder men coveted her and sought her attention. This attribute she was well aware of and used it to her benefit immensely. She mocked them as she knew that all they saw was her face, not her heart. Her emotions had died long back, and she was living in the ruins of the past. She recklessly gave all of herself and then walked away from each relationship. Nothing truly mattered to her. They did not matter. All these reckless affairs with men held no relevance. She devoured men by enticing them, making them fall for her and then abandoning. This was her form of revenge. This was the new Maya. A Maya who did not dare to glare at her reflection in the mirror and question herself. The human mind suffers in varied ways as our reactions to divergent situations are different. Life will throw that curveball. It's how you duck and fight the bad that determines you.

Ten minutes into the stillness of the night, a few streets beyond beckons her to this bar in the Argentinian city of Rosario where she performs a Milonga every night. Milonga is a form of tango, a dance form she learnt early to earn a living. Fifteen minutes away from the same Mark walks like a bewitched man, wearing his Sunday best attire, a pin-striped cravat, a crisp white shirt, black baby cord trousers and patent black shoes. His hair gelled, combed and in place. He is tall and handsome with an aquiline nose, a sharp jawline, and sinewed arms. Mark smelled fresh of citrus. All for Maya. Maya who will dance three scores with him. Not more. Maya whose waist his fingers will graze. Maya whose limpid grey eyes steal his vision. Maya stakes claim to all he holds in his heart.

Mike saw much more in Maya than what meets the eye. He saw her inner beauty and softness that reflected in her sad eyes. In an obscure moment of weakness, she had shown her loving nature when he once slipped and hurt his knee. He knew she had a kinder side beneath this harsh face she showed. For him, she wore a mask of a vile woman and Mike was determined to discover the Maya he knew existed behind that fallacy. He was an acclaimed Doctor of Clinical Psychology and had left his practise after his wife died of cancer. He had money to sustain him. He saw a beautiful woman in her who was capable of loving and caring and deeply too. He would soon discover for he like the others was enamoured but by what lay inside her mind.

Maya looks at Mike, as she saw, most men. Somewhere when her guard was down she admitted that she did find him attractive and liked to float in his arms and dance. She was fighting her own demons. The villains of her love. Though this she discards delicately every night, Yes every night she coquettishly entices and then leaves her scent lingering on his senses.

Three dances. Three dances is all she grants. He wonders at his passion and at the woman who he knows nothing of beyond this moment and the scattered incidences trivial in some way.

The chanteuse into the night sang the crescendo with fervour and clang. The dancers moved to an appassionato and arching their supple backs, they grove. Maya's dress a silvery shimmer, caught the light and glimmered and men gasped, and women envied. Her sensuous gliding moves on pulsating sounds made heartbeat resound in the bar. Her hips in rhythmic gentle sways were followed by whispers from the guests. Lustful eyes resided on her face. She kindled flames into her dance. She smiled at Mark and it reached her eyes. Mark seized the moment when sweetness sang into her face and he stayed entranced. Their eyes locked briefly.

In a hypnotic sensual synchronised dance- they entwined passionately with musicality in movement. Their senses swirl and soft tendrils from her chignon escape as he glides his fingers on her nape. Maya and Mike to an ocho align as they walk this dancing embrace. She twirls to end the crescendo with a whirl, her soft hands held firm in his. The last dance of the three.

Till one day she fell seriously ill and Mike called upon her and insisted on taking care of her. With that came a change of heart. That one month saw her soften and reveal her gentle demeanour and she cried again both with a relief of getting rid of her pain and exterior and with finding love again. Love can be a villain, yet love can be beautiful and can be all emotions of splendour and beauty.

Maya today sits to recap and calls it an aberration in her life. She gently combs her daughter's long hair and prays that true love befalls her. She sighs as she prepares a candlelit dinner table for her romantic husband who she adores and the demons of yore she sympathetically relegates to her past. Mike has made her wiser about forgiving and forgetting.

Robert falls in love with a lovely woman, who ironically is not a victim of his dalliance. She works hard to understand his mental state and seeks medical help to aid him. So, all's well murmurs Cupid as he roams with his arrow and sighs as he sees no villains in lovers lores.

16

THE RUTHLESS RATTLER

by Tulsi Nambiar

He rattled inside his cage, he wanted to be free. But his mistress suppressed him as had become the routine. It had been too long since he was free. The last time he was let free it was the most amazing time of his life. He wanted more of that; he wanted his freedom back. His hunger for freedom was increasing as time was passing him by. He had tried, really tried to 'calm down' as his mistress called it but he just couldn't, the darkness around him made it even harder. He wasn't made to keep quiet in a cage but was made to damage. His mistress was very biased. She let some of the other creatures out of their cages but not his and this only made him crave for freedom even more. His urge was unavoidable after all that's who he was. Sometimes when he gave up hope he would sit and think about his childhood.

Almost 20 years ago was when he was born as a little red ball. He was born in a cage, he was born with no freedom, as a slave. What was the necessity of freedom when you are a baby? But things change as you grow. When he was young he did not grow much. He remained a small red ball for a long time. It was the blue and yellow balls near him who grew, he was cross with his mistress, Sandra, for she never paid any attention to him. But slowly as time progressed his mistress started to nurture him. He felt a sense of satisfaction but not enough because something was missing. When he turned 9 something happened that changed his mistress's life. Her mother passed away and her father blamed her for it. But she thought it would pass but it didn't. She became closer to the blue ball which was turning into the size of a rock. Sandra's father made it very difficult for her to live, she thought about running away from her house many times but would get held up by sentimental attachments. When she turned 10 she had had enough of letting the blue rock out of its cage, she moved to the red baby rock. He was let out once in a while. That was freedom when he was let out to fly. He caused a lot of damage but that's what gave him the feeling he was missing – ecstasy. After a few times of flying his mistress realised the damage that was being done. So, she locked him up again. But once you know how to fly how can you stop? He begged to be free and promised lesser damage than last time even though he knew that was not a promise he could keep. His mistress was a lot stronger than she looked, he couldn't underestimate her. He needed to find new tricks.

Sandra soon turned 12, a dangerous age where a girl's emotions are not easy to read. She was confused but that was not all. Her father was still giving her a tough time. She tried to please him but Sandra was starting to look just like her mother which made things worse. Her father was becoming an alcohol addict if that wasn't obvious already! Sandra had to fend for herself just so she could have a decent meal. Her father stopped going to work and a lot of responsibilities were thrown her way which she was not ready for. But she handled it but what she didn't know was the red rock inside her cage was getting a lot bigger, almost as big as a boulder. Sometimes she could feel her ivory skin turn red, but she let it pass. When she turned 13 Sandra was no more able to control him. The red- boulder-like-bird flew further than he should have gone. He crashed into his mistress's father and there would be massive fights and then came the blue bird's turn to crash inside Sandra. But

Sandra was sometimes chaotic and was soon talking to a counsellor from school. That is when all the cages inside of her found their names. She had identified them finally after a long time. She soon started learning how to be a mistress. She learned to control the cages and their creatures and stopped letting them control her. This only caused more damage inside her. The red odd-shaped creature had had enough. He couldn't handle being controlled and he made sure that he was the one who controlled his 'mistress'. When the red creature was let out of its cage all hell broke loose, Sandra was soon seen as a monster among her peers. But that only encouraged him to cause more damage. It gave him the feeling he craved for – ecstasy. She shivered sometimes after her outbursts at the people around her. The worst part was that she blamed herself instead of blaming him. He took every opportunity he got in those two years to fly and make his mistress's life worse than it already was.

Soon Sandra turned 16 and she soon liked being called the monster of her class. Her red creature was now a common feature and she liked it. He was close to achieving his aim. The red creatures across the world are born with one aim to turn their masters and mistresses into feared monsters. He flew to places he had never seen before. He attained self-satisfaction that would soon go away and turn into hunger. He was always hungry for more even when his mistress had had enough he would want more. His mistress stopped trying to control him because she just couldn't. She made many attempts but all of them were failed missions. She always tried the hardest ways and forgot to use the easiest way to control him. Soon he was the master, and she was his slave even though it was supposed to be the other way around. The beast inside her was what everybody saw, not the hurt young child inside her. The red creature had painted her red from the outside and it was so thick a coat that nobody could get through. Now he had the biggest cage among the three of them.

When she turned 19 the red creature inside of her had become big enough to cover her whole body. All that she had against her father came out that night. It was her mother's 10th death anniversary. Her father was as usual unconscious because of alcohol. The red creature flew out and boom! It was as fast as lightning. The sight was disturbing. Sandra had lost consciousness but the red creature inside her was enjoying the feeling of victory. He had succeeded, he had lived to his purpose. He brought out the monster inside her, the ruthless creature that everyone tries to suppress. He had brought it out. He rose high as he saw Sandra's father's dead body lying on the floor with at least 15 stabs in the guts. The carpeted floor was bloody and filthy. Sandra came back to her senses; she was finding it hard to digest the sight in front of her. But somewhere inside of her, there was satisfaction. "After everything, he did to me he deserved this. After everything he put me through he deserved this." She pushed away these thoughts. It hit her that she had just killed her very own father in a ruthless way. She was ashamed and that is when she realised she had surrendered herself to the red creature inside of her. She finally said his name out loud. RAGE!!! She started screaming and tried to run away. But she couldn't move because her feet were rooted. Rage was clearly the master. He roared as loudly as he could. He made her feel powerless, the way he felt as a child. He soared above her and showed her what he was capable of. Sandra was motionless, the colour from her face was draining. He attained eternal ecstasy as he slowly went back inside her. The blue creature, SADNESS wanted to help but she could do nothing for Sandra. She was thinking of her mother, her beautiful face with kindness in her eyes but that had all disappeared. When her mother was alive there were two other creatures inside of her, which were big and bold, LOVE and HAPPINESS. But after her mother died Rage and Sadness had killed the other two creatures. She felt empty like everything inside her was gone. There was nothing but a gut-wrenching pain inside her body. The beast inside of her had come out. Now there was nothing but darkness inside her. She embraced the darkness inside her for that was who she was.

She no longer had to worry about what people thought of her for that she had done the worst possible. She committed one of the most unforgivable crimes in this world. But she blamed her father for it. If only he had treated her right maybe life wouldn't have been like this. She went through the same pain as him maybe even worse, but he only blamed her for what happened. Natural death was out of her control, but murder wasn't. It felt good to be free. She had never experienced this feeling before, it felt amazing. The darkness inside of her was what really brought light into her life. Now it would be the darkness that guided her life. She no longer needed her emotions. She was going to get rid of them. They were placed in the darkest corner of her body, the heart, they would never see light again. Rage would never know of his fate; he would never know that he was the only prisoner inside her. Sadness had disappeared like all the other emotions who were no more there. Rage felt like others were being let out while he was locked up. But he was the only one inside. It was all his imagination. No one ever saw Sandra again and no one had any knowledge of what had happened to her father. She was a mystery, a dark mystery to the outside world. But she was happy and free inside her darkness. Embracing the darkness inside her gave her what she wanted most – Freedom.

17

SUBLIME EXISTENCE

by Pritha Shyam

Rishav

Rishav startled and woke as the blazing sound of the aircraft tortured his ears. It has been a long flight, and he could not remember when his eyes closed. After a span of 8 long years, he was in his homeland, yet he could feel the reluctance in his veins. His last residing place was Ireland- but he would not call it home. HOME to him was in the dingy lanes of Dumdum in the city of joy when the din and bustle of the slum life woke him up. How he used to identify all the varying sounds that surrounded him!- Pinky Kakima's pressure cooker whistling away, Polash Kaku's brushing and gurgling sound, the chatter at the 'water tap queue' (which would someday turn into a full-fledged quarrel), the sound of the factory nearby, Bhola the street dog barking away...he wanted to hear them all...all over again...except for a voice- a voice which he so fiercely hated that for a moment he regretted to have arrived in this city for attending a seminar. As he got down from the flight, he could have the waft of the unique scent of Kolkata, and as soon as he was on the taxi on the way to his hotel, nostalgia engulfed him.

Kalyani

Today was another new day, or was it? To the shrunken body of the 48-year-old Kalyani, it was not something new, but another call pulling her closer to the end. She knew it was inevitable, and yet her smile never left her face. The fear of dying alone terrified her, so she had her best friend by her side, Kamala, who knew what she had gone through. Her room was right by the station, and she loved interacting with whosoever went by- but she mostly replied with disgust, and very rarely one would actually respond to her. But even then, she had constant companions apart from Kamala- Kaloo, the coolie who came by whenever he got the time, and the stationmaster Praneeth Babu, who lovingly called her Jethima. Apart from that, she would talk endlessly with the street children who went in and out of the station and told them stories. She had her own reasons for choosing this room right beside the station, and the only thing that would disturb her would be the sudden sound of the superfast express trains when she would sit up and ask, - "keo elo?" (did anyone come?).

Rishav

"The night has been good!- I have got my fill of vengeance...though temporarily"- Rishav thought. Kaloo had selected the perfect girl and brought her over, and he had beaten the shit out of her and violated her the entire night. Kaloo's contact was given to him by one of Rishav's colleagues who had described him as - "A perfect pimp in the disguise of a Coolie". Rishav had always felt a sadistic pleasure in violating call girls brutally and it had nothing to do with his sexual needs. He hated them...all of them. It was not that he had not been rough with girls back in Ireland, but he wanted to have his way with an Indian prostitute. Rishav woke in the morning and opened the window followed by a grin on his face. This is exactly what he has been missing. From the top floor of the Peerless Inn, he could feel his incredible love for the din and bustle of Kolkata, not any city, but this one. His thoughts were interrupted by the bell on his door and a staff peeping in- "Sir your complimentary breakfast is ready, you can have Chinese, Italian, Mexican, anything you please."

"That won't be necessary thank you." He smiled and left off. Just as he crossed Lindsay Street, a familiar smell of hot Kachoris and curry lured him, and he said- "Well this is the kind of breakfast that would soothe me now!" and ordered a plateful.

All of a sudden he could not help but feel tears trickling down his cheek. "She used to make Kachoris on my birthday.....NO! But I hate that person! I would never see that face again let alone eat something from that hand!" He gritted his teeth in anger and even when the hot plate of kachoris was placed in front of him, his appetite ebbed away. He paid for the plate and left.

Kalyani

By the time it was evening, Kalyani's condition had worsened. Right after breakfast, she had coughed out blood and her body felt warm. The fever had been recurring and Kamala was worried. She began frothing from her mouth in the evening and Praneeth Babu called the doctor immediately. All that escaped her lips before losing consciousness was- "find him....take him to me". The doctor examined and all he could say was- "I think it's time...if there is anyone she wants to meet, it's time you called..". As soon as he said this, the frantic search began. Praneeth Babu and Kaloo learnt everything from Kamala and went out- he was determined to find him no matter what.

Rishav

"Damn it! Why won't this Kaloo pick up the call... bloody idiot..", Rishav was visibly annoyed.

After several times, Kaloo picked up the phone, only to say that he would not be able to turn up. When Rishav asked why he could just answer that his maashi was dying and he needed to find someone for her.

"Listen Kaloo, I will pay you extra, just get me what I need, and you can be on your stupid search ok?"

That night when Kaloo came, he had a girl with him, just like the way Rishav wanted- nubile yet innocent, and yet Kaloo's face was what Rishav noticed first. It was dark and it seemed like he had been out all day. Neither did he ask for the money, nor did he have the lecherous look in his eyes. Something made his heart stagger and he asked Kaloo…

"Who is it that you are so worried about? You said someone was dying?…is it your family?

"I don't have any family babu, and this maashi is more than family to me. She scolds me for the sideline business I do, but how much can you actually earn from being a coolie? Hunger brings me in these dark alleys"

"Well, you should try something else Kaloo"

"That's what Kalyani maashi says too! But easier said than done na babu…"

For a moment, Rishav's head spun, and he felt the ground being swept away from under his feet.

"What name did you say again? Kaloo speak up!"- he yelled.

"…Kal..Kalyani maashi…but why do you ask babu…"

"Who was she searching for?"

"Kamaladi said she wanted to see Rishubaba"

"GET OUT! GET OUT OF HERE NOW BEFORE I KILL YOU- AND ASK THE BITCH TO DIE", Rishav spat out.

As the door closed, Kaloo was shocked to realise the naked truth- "Rishubaba and Rishav sir was the same individual"- and as soon as it struck him, he ran for his life to tell Kalyani that he had found what she wanted.

Kalyani

Kalyani had just gained her senses, but she was too weak to talk. She was gasping for air when she spoke and yet, she had a lot to speak about.

Kamala was straining her ears to understand every word she said the first of which were-

"Have you found him?"

"No didi, we haven't but we will, promise."

"You don't understand, it's late, I don't have much time"

"Don't say this please"- Kamala said teary-eyed.

"Will you do something for me? Pick the flowerpot outside the door and bring the box you see"

Kamala did the same and when she opened it, she found a number of tablets in there.

"Didi! Esob ki! (what is this!)- all this time you have been fooling us by saying you took the meds while all that you did was to keep them hidden under the pot? Why did you do this didi? Why?

"Kamala, this is a cursed life you see.....the earlier I leave, the better....and the one I loved most, hates me...what's the use of this wretched life, can you tell me?

In the meantime, Kaloo barged in panting- "aami take peyechi (I got him! I got him!)"

"Who did you get Kaloo, who...Rishubaba?" she could hardly breathe... "where is he? What did he say?" she tried to peek out of the door...thinking there must be someone.

Kaloo's enthusiasm died as soon as he heard the questions and started stammering

"Your Rishubaba...Rishav sir..he is so caring...was asking about you...cried when I said you wanted to meet him....you know he travels by flight now!...staying in such a big hotel!", Kaloo was trying to divert the topic in any manner he could.

"No need to lie Kaloo, I know he wished my death. I know my son far more than you ever will"- she smiled at Kamala- "You know sister, I took this place near the station and waited beside this window waiting for him- because I wanted to become the first person to welcome him as soon as he would step in the platform searching for me...I could never understand that he would grow so big that he would travel by flight...silly me. Kamala, will you do another thing for me? The last I promise"

"Yes didi"

"Take the Bhagavad Gita out of my drawer and flip it- you would find a piece of paper...give it to Kaloo. Will you give it to Rishubaba for me Kaloo?

All she could hear was the muffled cries. As the morning dawned and a little bird fluffled on the windowsill, Kalyani took her last breath.

That night, he violated the call girl in a way that the only thing left was to kill her. He spat on her and threw a bundle of notes on her body and told her to leave- and she was still crying when she did what was told.

The next morning, the striking sound of the ambulance woke him up and he ran to the window. He knew she could be in any one of these ambulances passing by- or maybe not. The sound of the crowd which had seemed too welcoming to him was like a poison to his ears. He wanted everything to stop for a while- he hated that person and yet felt restless by the news. He retched and retched in the washroom and cried in the corner clasping his knees to his chest after the girl had gone off- and yet he knew not why.

After hours, when he felt a bit sane, he frantically searched for his cell phone and dialled Kaloo's number. All he could hear on the other side was a sob which ended with - "Are you happy now Rishav Sir? The BITCH is dead, just as you wished".

The next hours were blurry for Rishav and he does not remember when and how he could reach the stinking lanes of Sealdah. As he stood in front of the 'body'- his Kalyani maa, he could feel his insides shattering into a thousand pieces....and he desperately wanted to travel back in time. All of a sudden he felt a hand on his shoulder and felt a piece of paper being tucked into his palm by Kaloo. He started reading....

THE LETTER

Rishubaba,

If you are reading this letter, then probably I am no longer in this world. I have wanted to tell you so much since you left, but I know I would never be lucky enough to meet you again. Luck..this is the word that God forgot to jot down in my life I guess..yet he gave me a treasure like you...so I am leaving with no complaints whatsoever. I understand that a eunuch should have no complaints- they are born to drag their way to death. But I was not born this way Rishav- I was just a simple lad in a middle-class family, going to school, playing with other kids- until puberty hit me...and I realised I was a girl trapped in a male body. The school bell which seemed so amazing to me started seeming like a nightmare- when the other kids started treating me like an utter alien. I was born Kalyan...but I was one of the numerous mistakes by God...and I started treating myself as Kalyani- trying mother's saree and decking up when no one was around. I was a shame to the family, they said and when I was 15, I was driven out by my parents. With whatever education I had gained by then, I wanted to look for work, I was determined not to "clap around", not to "beg". A proper job is again something which is not meant for eunuchs- until I found the man who actually wanted to love me and give me shelter. I was one hell of a fool, I must say...When I realised what kind of work he had in store for me, I was already immersed in the quicksand of the red-light alleys of Sobhabazar...a place with no escape route. Apparently, Eunuchs too, have a great demand there, and I was one of the most 'demanded' eunuchs for my sharp features. See the irony Rishu? I fled from 'clapping and begging' only to become a "prostitute". I spent 12 years in that hell-hole all alone wanting to die until the day YOU crawled into my life....I still had to go back to the hell hole, but now I had someone to fight for...

I still remember the day when Kamala and I were getting back from the bazaar and we saw you- merely a three-month-old baby crying your lungs out- but nobody noticed you. Not far off we could see a crashed car, in which probably your parents lay dead. Kamala had tried to tug me off, but as soon as I held you in my arms, I knew I could not leave you. That day I realised that not only did I have a girl trapped inside me, but that girl had also grown out to be a mother in all these years". I sneaked you out of the spot, but I was determined not to let you be in the stench of the dark. That is why I rented a space in Dumdum where I would guard you all day long and leave as soon as you slept. I am sorry babu, for all those nights I couldn't be with you, for not taking you to school and bringing you back- I know you had endless questions and all I could give you in return was silence. But I guess, how much ever I wanted you to remain small, you had to grow big - big enough to understand everything that I have been hiding. I knew you had followed me to find out where I worked and that is exactly the moment you started feeling the disgust for me- you never had the guts to tell me- but a mother always knows...

The last time I saw you was when I was being ushered into the police van with some other pimps and workers of the red-light area and I would never forget the hatred in your eyes. The only thing that I wanted to shout out was I was the one who tipped the police regarding underage human trafficking and saved 12 innocent lives- but you left thinking of me as the convict...never to return again. I used to hear things about you getting a scholarship and leaving Kolkata, but that is all I could gather. Remember the flower that you planted Rishu when you were in the sixth standard? That is still with me babu- I have taken care of it as if it were you...I know you will hate me, even more, when you know the disease that I have died from- AIDS...But now that I am gone, you will no longer have anyone to hate...no matter where I am, I will keep on loving you- just like I did when I cradled you for the first time. I knew eunuchs had a volatile existence- we burn to live and abruptly die one day- and I have proved it right with my life. Stay blessed.

With lots of cares,

Kalyani Maa,

The unfortunate eunuch who could not hear "maa" for the last time.

"MAA! Get up ma!! Just this last time maa....just this once- I will never leave you again maa...A mother can never be always right maa....You were so so wrong. I do not hate you because you died of AIDS.... See I have come for you. Ma, please get up, just this once!"- all anyone could hear was the desperate sobs and shrieks of Rishav which emanated out of his wounded, grief-stricken, guilty heart.

Later on, as Rishav put her shrouded body on his shoulders, his eyes fell on the flowerpot, which had withered with Kalyani- and he could find himself languishing without her existence...such is the sublimity of life.

18

RECKLESS

by Ravgun Kaur

Unblinking eyes started into mine. They weren't wide open, rather the upper lids reached about halfway to meet the lower ones, almost like a drunken serenity. I was expecting them to blink anytime now, not looking elsewhere; not even at the new colour that seemed to adorn her otherwise pink lips, the deadly stale brown which I felt mixing into my bloodstream and travelling straight to my lungs.

I let out a foul breath. Keeping my eyes pried open for a minute straight, I leaned forward without breaking my stare so that I didn't miss anything in case we were blinking in sync. But her unmoving eyes continued to shoot accusations at mine.

I scoffed, "I didn't do anything."

I still remember the day she passed that driving test and surprised me with a honk outside my window. We drove around town yelling "I've got a car, suckers!" or in my case "She's got a car, suckers!" We made a lot of stops just to dramatically exit the car, the concrete under our sneakered feet stood like solid freedom. We refused to go back home that day - the goal was to run out of fuel, and have it refilled just to 'see what it feels like', but our parents yelling over the phone was enough to get us to cancel all plans and rush home like our asses were on fire.

I skipped dinner because of all the chocolate bars I'd stuffed throughout the day and went straight to my room, unable to get the wide smile off my face. That night, when the day's sounds buzzing in my ears were slowly fading with a decrease in adrenaline, a new voice echoed in my head as I fell asleep "She's got a car before you, sucker".

My soiled dress brushed against my bruised knee as I limped with one hand on Lainey's shoulder (I liked to call her Lainey, short for Elaine, but she would get very upset about how it wasn't a pretty name. So, I called her Lainey in my head and Elaine when she could hear me). Her silver tiara shone over her head. It had rained in the morning and the Sun was now out, shining on her very generously as her dark brown curls, that appeared lighter under the sunshine and made her seem even more radiant than she already was, fell to meet her shoulders adorned in glittery sleeves of her pink dress that flowed to her feet.

That night I dreamt of a distant memory.

Her shoes were dirty though, from when she helped me get up after I'd tripped in the playground. My own tiara was in my schoolbag and my hair was tied back from when the teacher had to wash my muddy face. We were walking towards my mommy who was smiling at me from a distance, but a frown made way between her eyebrows as we got near. She bent down, inspected me from head to toe and all the while I was wishing I looked pretty like Lainey, who stood by on her tiptoes, waiting to wave me goodbye before I left, rolling left to right, then right to left, then left to right, her tiara still glimmering, curls bouncing, green eyes shining. I was mesmerised.

I left soon after my mommy smiled at Lainey and patted her on the head, her frown long gone now. Then she picked me up and buckled me inside the car - the image of Lainey's light pink dress swarming inside my head throughout the whole drive as my silent tears stained mine even more.

Now that I think about it, her eyes never lost that stupid shine. It was always there when we were dressed as princesses in kindergarten, when drove around the city in her car, when she celebrated her sweet sixteen and the candle wax ruined her cake because she couldn't come up with a wish, when she went out on her first date - not before driving over to my place to ask how she looked. My mom freaked out when she reversed out of the driveway, almost knocking the trashcan down in the process, yelling, "Sorry I have to make it back home before he arrives and then pretend I just came out of my room", before zooming off, her last word still lingering in the silence she left behind.

She always left such an aftertaste of a horrid hush that would cause you to curse her presence.

Just like I was cursing it now. Oh, how I hated her presence from the start!

I scoffed again, "She had always been reckless with cars."

And then she got her first job, while I was still babysitting my aunt's daughter for some cash because my mom who thought I was "too naïve" wouldn't let me leave town. So, there I sat with a degree in my hands, hoping I could finally prove myself to be better than Elaine (I called her Elaine in my head now and Lainey when she could hear me). She moved away in the city perhaps because she was capable enough in her mother's eyes, and maybe in my mothers' eyes too. And that was what I asked Lainey when she came to visit us,

"Am I stupid?" only to see the most perplexed expression on her face.

"Why would you ask that?"

"My mom won't let me move to the city."

"I'll talk to her."

And she did, immediately she talked to my mom, who on being convinced by 'Elaine', not-so-surprisingly agreed to send me to live with her for two weeks and if things went smoothly, would let me move. So, the next evening I was done packing my bags and we loaded them into the back of her car. My mom packed us some snacks for the road and we set out. I still can hear Don't Stop Believin' merged with Elaine's voice echoing in my head, her hair grazing the headrest as she swayed her head to the song, closing her eyes during the high notes, laughing when I fussed about how she should keep her eyes on the road.

And soon she had gotten me out of the small town and brought me into the city. But you see, I never asked her to talk to my mom. I only asked her if I was stupid. And she never answered.

I scoffed, "Ever so reckless while driving."

But I made it. I worked day and night, much to Elaine's perturbation, and moved out. I got a good job, got my own place, had my own friends but above all I had something of hers, something she was carrying on her ring finger, studded on rounded metal, and sparkling like the green in her eyes. I had a man who, like every other thing, she had gotten before me. It was then I realised that I wasn't lesser but late. And I had to tell her that.

Tiny shards of glass adorned the driveway, and I relished the thought of teary green eyes, shining for completely different reasons very soon. He had refused to tell her about us. "Do it yourself", he said, but you see, it just had to come from him. So, I left a note on his behalf on the windshield of her car that I'd showered with the blows of my secret envy. Feeling lighter, I'd driven back home thinking that if he wouldn't come out to her, I could send her to him.

But instead of driving a few blocks away to meet him, she had decided to cross half the city to where I'd found a home far away from her place. Unable to trust that note, she had come to see me first. And she decided to drive there in a car with broken headlights. Headlights that I'd broken.

I scoffed one last time at the dull green eyes looking at me in the morgue before making my way home.

She was so reckless and stupid.

"Reckless.." I grumbled to myself.

"Reckless.." My hand tightened on the steering wheel.

"Reckless.." I whispered as I shifted the gears.

"Reckless.." I stepped on the gas.

"Reckless.." I turned the wheel.

"Stupid Lainey." I drove off the bridge.

19

A TWILIGHT REVERE

by Shreya Shenoy

It's twilight. The four walls of this confinement are coming closer. Closer and closer. I close my eyes. Darkness envelops me, throwing hard iron shackles and I am trapped. A high-pitched scream pierces the dusk. At a distance, a hound reciprocates. Soon, the moon will peek through the monsoon clouds that do not spare even the night sky, to listen to the silent gossip that goes on in the surrounding forest. But I await the arrival of the silent presence of the symbol of love. The moonlight in whose glory, the lovers bask, burns me. The wind outside is the remnant of the storm that brewed in me. Yet, for a soul that has known nothing but darkness, the company is welcome. The smell of wildflowers that drifts to me from the forest reminds me of freedom, of the life I should have had. The petrichor from the drops that recently escaped the sky, fills my heart with the unwelcome emotion. Love. I had long forsaken it. It has been my foe since the day we set eyes on each other. Though today, he is a long-lost nemesis.

Among all this, I watch the shy shade of the setting sun reminding me of the rosy bloom of the woman I once loved. Behind iron clad bars of this godforsaken place, as I watch the blue of the sky plunge into the depth of black. Like my soul did not so long ago.

For both of us, the pink of health was not so healthy after all. Clock ticks in a rhythm, I have always despised. Nature takes her breath-taking creativity and draws the most magnificent night that has come in a long while. Yet, the twinkling stars remind me of the time her eyes used to dazzle with excitement. The stardust scattered over the horizon compares nothing to the joy she had spread in my silent survival. Life was bliss just like this night.

All this seems an eon away. From a life I had before these rotten grey walls became the boundaries of my existence and my life drenched in the hues of red and black. When I close my eyes, all I remember is that wretched day.

The day I killed for the love of my life.

It was a dark summer's night. There was excitement in the air. The kind that the lion feels when it is about to hunt. The sound of church bells reminding me, it is time. After days of preparation, the day had finally arrived. I had the routine memorised and my act planned. I wasn't going to let anything go wrong with it. Because for the first time in my life, I was capable of protecting what is mine. Unlike all these years of deprivation. And there he was having dinner in the small café of the locality. The revolver in my pocket could feel the quiver that ran through me. I waited for the arrival of my prey as patient as the lion king. Bidding goodbye to his friends, he began walking towards me. Yes. Carpe diem.

The underrated chloroform and my hanky is all I used to get him where I wanted. In the back alley of her apartment. As I waited for him to come round, I had flashes.

I was 4, my father had just told me my mother died. No. How could she? She was my angel. I was her little boy. Her knight. I remember being so helpless.

I was 6, my dad got a new mommy home. She's like the evil stepmother of the fairy in my book. She makes me clean her room when daddy is at work. If I don't, she beats me with the whip.

I was 8, Step mommy has a new baby, she gives him my doll. But I love my teddy. I try to snatch it back. He is my teddy; you don't touch him. Go away. No...No...

I was 16, that wretched lady burnt my garage. It had all my memories. Now I have nothing. Today, I will give her a taste of her own medicine. I remember hiding her whip under my T-shirt and hiding under her bed. She caught me and threw me out of the house.

That was the day I met him. The one I hide like my very own brother. My demon. All the good force of the world would kneel before him. I brewed him with all the deadly poisons from the apothecary of life. He grew stronger and stronger. Until...

Until the day I met her.

It's time. He is coming round. Time to get the show on the road.

"Well. Well. Look who is here. My dear dear Alfred."

"Who are you? What do you want? Let me go ." Poor Alfred. Shouldn't have courted my Sarah.

"Each time I look at you, I see her. My Sarah. You make her unhappy. You creep!"

"What! I did nothing."

"Struggling with these ropes is not going to help this situation. Tonight, I am going to make my Sarah happy. I am going to rid this world of filth like you."

"Let me go!"

"Now don't get all innocent. I know who you are. I know you are playing her."

Two years after the day I was thrown out of my paternal accommodation, I had managed to create a new identity. I was working in a company. Doing odd jobs, running errands. It helped to keep my demon at bay. And at night I let him out unleased him and learnt to fight and kill.

"And today, I get to use all the training on you. Haha."

My boss from the company was a man of many faces. A well-known lawyer, a businessman and the guardian of the underworld. He ran a hundred businesses legally and a million others illegally. A true gangster hiding the monster behind his gentleman's suit. Being a lawyer, he used his knowledge to prey on the wealthy and help the worst criminals get away.

I was handed a new project the day I met Sarah. And she was yar. The lowly assistant as I was, I never gathered the courage to talk to her. Days passed and I was living my life on cloud nine. Her smile, her eyes were ever-present on my subconscious. I never thought of my undercover Mr. Jenkel or even Dr. Hyde. She was my talisman.

A few days later I discovered she was meeting with another gentleman to be married and my life shattered like the wall mirror. It had become my routine to watch her, so I did that day too. And then I saw him. The bastard. My boss, Alfred.

"I discovered from work; you are going to use her as the alibi for your next gangster. And I will not let you. Today marks the end of your lifetime of crimes."

"Help. Let me go"

I had my revolver ready. I put it on his temple.

"Yes! Yes! I am playing her. Now let me go".

"So easy for you to say. Today, I want you to scream for your life. Come on now, be a sport, let me hear it."

And he screamed. And she came running.

The demon was at the start line. Breaking the shackles of civility, he stood all high and mighty. Eyes red, gut-wrenching hatred spurred through each cell of my body. Tonight is the day of revenge. Today, I will help what is mine. Today, I will save what is mine. I could see the face of my stepmother loom over him and that was it.

Shot no.1

"NO!" She screamed. Tonight, Sarah's screams won't stop me.

Shot no.2 and it went straight into his heart splattering red over the black wall. The demon in me was awake. It has seen blood, the battlefield it wanted was created.

3, 4, 5 and all the blood in his body was a fertilizer to the soil.

"You sick piece of shit!" It was Sarah. She was really here. "I loved him. What have you done?" And she started to cry. And my existence began to melt away.

"Sarah, I…"

"Shut up! You lowly creature. You have not known one shred of love in your life and you choose to murder my love? How could you?

How will I live now?

Oh, Alfred! My happily ever after lies here, all drenched in cold red blood

Why will I live now?"

With strange determination, she stood and with a swift movement snatched my revolver and shot.

Right over her temple.

There is a knock on the door interrupting my revere. And he's awake. Like the eye of the storm for a split second I remain calm, try hard to contain him. Futile. From the depths of a sinking pit, arises smoke as though from a fire burning on the fuel of anger, revenge, and hatred. The deadly trio of destruction. As the smoke rises and frees itself from my efforts, there I feel him. The demon. Splitting through the darkness, I see red. There is an eruption of the familiar emotion, he is close. Breaking the shackles, he is out. And I scream. This time out of fury. My limbs are out of control. I want to rip apart things. I … want… to… kill. I want to burn and run. The demon is ready and stomping his feet. I speak out incomprehensible words and shout. I want to rip out my own vocal cords and then the door opens. There are people facing me, the demon and he's bloodthirsty. Today, I will reign this battle. My gut desires the flesh of these horrendous beings. They approach me, cautiously there are 3 of them and my demon is hungry. Shouting, I launch myself at them. The demon laughs seeing them struggle to contain him. The cold, high pitched laugh and I calculate their moves. A fourth person comes running with something in his hand and strikes me. Anger turns to annoyance to pain and I collapse.

When I wake up, my world is set right. I am behind the now-familiar bars. There is moonlight in my room and there is no sign of him. Maybe, he is gone.

But I know it's an empty hope. Tomorrow, when the dusk bids goodbye and twilight takes the main stage, he will be back.

And I will see her again.

Sleep bewitches me, taking me to the bizarre world of dreams. Today I will endure it, until time decides to put me to sleep, eternally.

20

SECRET AND SIN

by Mayuri Kashyap

SECRET

"Don't do this" were the last words I heard from my mother.

"This is a sin, God will punish you..!!" my father shouted from behind, as he came close to me with teary eyes.

"No Dad, I am not going to sacrifice my struggle for you all." I shouted back.

"Why don't you understand? What you are asking for is not possible!" My father sighed as my mother began to cry again.

"I have told you! I can't live here with you people.. I'm tired of this. I want to live my life." I shouted at him as I went into my room to collect my things.

I slammed the door and slid down to the floor and I rested my head on the door. I heard my father shouting for me to open the door, with my mother's weeps.

"This is wrong... I won't let you go... Calm down..." Were the only voices which came in.

I had expected nothing much from them - just a little support, a little money to live my dreams, that's all I had wanted. To work as a normal human, to be able to go to school and college, to work, to talk to people, to make friends, to live. And he can't even let me do this.

I had spent years trying to make him understand the kind of life I wanted, how much I wanted to study, and work. I was even ready to live alone, and that's what I am going to do now. If they wouldn't understand me I wouldn't understand them as well. Now I will do what I had planned for years. Now I will do whatever I want today was the last day I pleaded in front of him. Now all the hard work done will pay off. I value my dreams.

They were like this since forever, sacrificing all they had for others. But I won't be like them, I will leave even if it means that I have to kill somebody. I don't care.

I picked a few dresses which I had stolen from people who used to come to the beach. I had a pair of sunglasses which I had snatched from a girl whom I had to knock out. Haha, funny moments. There's that one pair of red heels I stole from another girl. I had really loved those heels when I saw them. I decided to have them, so I had it.

I picked up the keys I had hid among the mess. I had won it from a dealer after talking for a few days. That fool! he agreed to share his house with me, and stupidly gave me the keys. It was not difficult - just showing off some of my innocent looks and voila done. He melted like butter and gave his keys to me, what more can be expected from a horny ass like him. I seriously wonder where these humans will end one day.

But there was one thing, money!

I had no money in my pocket. I scooted to my cupboard to see if I had any money, and I scoured everywhere only to find a few coins.

By midnight I had collected all that I had wanted, and went to my sister's room, without making any sound. I opened her cupboard and just like I thought I found them. She always got the good gems and jewellery, now I can finally have them, I have always envied the way my parents treated her as if being the younger one comes with benefits of "Ohh let her have this one she is younger" card.

Now all her gems and diamonds lay in front of me, I picked everything from the drawer and her dressing table.

I crept to my parents' room, did the same. Speeding, I picked out every nickel and penny I could find.

I came to my room and took out a bag I stitched just for this day. It had a beach and sun embroidered on it. It took me years to make this bag.

Finally, the moment has come!

Finally, the night I can use this bag - to run away with the sun and me.

It was dawn when I had planned to leave my house. As I reached for the doorknob, my mother came with nothing but tears in her eyes. She never had anything to say, just like this time. I had always hated the fact that she never speaks, that she never shows any emotions, neither anger nor hurt. I wanted her to say something to me, something, anything, but she didn't. As she edged closer to hold my hand and drag me back to the room my eyes fell on the chain she was wearing. So, I did what my mind told me. I snatched it and pushed her. I saw her falling down as she fell on the floor with tears flowing from her eyes.

I asked her to keep quiet and ran. To live my life. Who cares what my family wants, or what is wrong and what is right. This is what I want for freedom.

I travelled, travelled away from that gutter, away from those people, so far that they wouldn't ever find where I live. And, finally, I reached my destination.

When I was finally there, my last task was left, my only step away from my freedom. I went to that man, with whom I was supposed to share the house. I went to him and spent a few days, unhurriedly poisoning him with my love and easily killing him with my body, and when he was finally head over heels for me I took my chance and ended him. Anyway, he was breathing with one foot in the grave, 70 years old. How long does one want to live?

Then I packed his bags and sent him to the place he belonged to. When the house was finally mine, I sat on the floor for hours, thinking about all I had done to acquire it.

The next few eons passed in a blur.

I stole from people, killed a few, anyway, they were greedy jerks who wanted to use me, so I used them. I thought about my mother the last time I had seen her, how her tears were asking me to stop, but I didn't. I know for sure, the next day my father must have taken the house on his head.

He must have slapped mother also, must have created a whole ruckus and commotion.

He was always like that, always dividing the world in right and wrong, always worrying, always fearing God. Who is God? Where is it? Who knows and who cares...!

I am free now, I want to live, and I will live. Tears started to well up in my eyes, but I wiped them before they could spill. I lay down on the floor looking at the ceiling, just gazing at it and planning what I needed to do next.

SHOPPING

PROCESSING

HIDING

LIVING

I went out and placed my order, the things which were needed to hide my secret.

It was 2 pm when I heard the knock on my door. I knew who it was. I couldn't help but smile.

"Your supplies," said the delivery boy.

"Thank you" I replied as I paid him the price and his commission.

"You have my number right, just give me a call if you need something," he said with a smile as his eyes travelled down my body. From my head to my feet. I followed his gaze, saw lust in his eyes.

I snatched the bag from his hands and shut the door on his face. This new house sucks. But I need this place, my sanctuary for a while. To hide my truths and to survive.

I went to the living room, closed every window, and drew every curtain down, Which I didn't really like personally. Some sunshine, some clouds, some blues, some stars are needed right? That's what tells you that nothing is constant in life. But I had to shut it all out. I used to love looking out of the windows and the sun rising, but I can't do it anymore. It's okay I have a rooftop to go and watch the sunrise. All mine.

I moved every furniture and pushed them close to the walls. Now I got the space, just below the fan and in front of the television cleared. I sat there for a few minutes in silence, living every moment of this new chapter of life. Then I emptied the package on the floor. Time to work now.

SHOVEL

GARDENING GLOVES

CHISEL

WATER POT

BOOTS

PIPE

I had even watched some videos and DIY tricks to do my work easily and quickly, like some silly little human. I had spent many hours on my research. When the sun was almost about to set, I picked up my weapons, rolled up my sleeves, rolled the carpet and kept it aside. I was hesitant to throw it as it may be needed afterwards to hide my secret.

I started to dig. I carved a rectangle on the floor, a few feet longer than me, a little broader and deep enough to hide me inside it completely.

After hard work of hours of digging, after using all my strength, by the time it was dark outside, I was done with the pit. I looked at my feet all muddy and sluggish, and my hands dirty up to elbows. The memory of all the creatures, worms, and bugs I met in this digging journey came in my mind. At this point, I know almost every kind of worm which lived under the ground. My white shirt is all brown now.

I looked at the time - it was almost midnight.

So, I got up from the floor, my legs shivered from all the hard work and my body ached after using all my strength.

But I had to do it. I picked the pipe from the floor attached to tap from the sink of the kitchen while making myself a sandwich to eat. After eating and catching my breath for a while, I began to work again.

When the pit was filled with water. I turned on the television, it only shows black and white dots as I haven't got the connection yet. Made myself a mint tea. And a few more sandwiches to eat with tea. I love this life, no disturbance, just laying and eating.

I opened some app, logged in for job hunting, got a few offers as well, in a restaurant, in a pub, and also applied for a college. I searched a lot on where I could get fake certificates. Got some tricks to do it but that can wait. For now, I just have to hide this truth.

When water almost started to spill out, I came out of my shirt and jumped in it. Coldwater relieves all the stress of hard work, relaxing my muscles. I wish I could open these curtains to see the stars, but this is my life now, this is how I have to live now, without skies and stars. As this is a life I choose for myself, after deceiving my family.

I let out a deep breath as I saw my reflection on the mirror kept near the television on the floor. Next to which was kept that bag, I sewed with sun and beach on it. I knew I needed a reminder of how my life was. Of how far I have come to live this dream, of how much I have sacrificed. I know I have made sins, wronged people, but what about the dreams, I stole from people only from those who had bad eyes on my jewellery, I killed those who harmed me, I deceived my family because they wanted that life, and I wanted this.

FREEDOM!

SECRETS!

HUMAN!

LIFE!

SIN!

"Humans," I said and looked down, to see my waving fins.

"Let's live this side of life," I said to myself and lunged into the water once again.

21

SAVED BY A SIREN

by C.L. Williams

Hironei was atop of a building, singing her song. It's the same song she has sung since Persephone was taken from Hades. The song was depressing; however, her angelic melodies would still attract men to her voice. Even after multiple millennia, she could still lure a man to his death. From atop the building Hironei sits upon to sing her song, she can see the entire city. She can see the changes man has made since her time on the island with her sisters. This world has more structures, everyone is looking down at something instead of speaking to their brothers and sisters, and the air isn't what it once was when she was on the island. Tonight was different, Hironei did not lure a man to his death. Tonight, Hironei played the role of a heroine.

Hironei sees a man near the building she is on top of and decides to start singing her song. She projects her voice into his direction, wanting to lure him to her. To Hironei's surprise, her song does not lure him. She's too high up to see why he isn't in a trance from her voice. For the first time in over a century, Hironei reveals her wings and flies down to the ground.

Hironei hides her wings before anyone notices, in this time, creatures like herself have been hunted and killed. She can't take any chances with humans anymore. She stretches out her wings, spanning over eight feet, her wings are white and have a bright glow to them. She lands on the ground behind the man and once again, releases her melody in his direction. To her surprise, he is not affected by her song. A confused Hironei walks closer to the man and tries to figure out why.

As Hironei gets closer to the man, she sees something covering his ears. Fearful that man has created an invention to prevent them from hearing her song makes her wonder how much longer her song will last. To Hironei's surprise, while she was trying to lure one man to his death, she sees that her song did indeed affect someone else and his death looks imminent. In most cases, Hironei would be ok with this man dying. This moment, she sees this man holding the hand of a little girl who looks scared. She sees that the little girl wants to scream, but fear has taken over and is leaving the little girl mute. She is pulling on the man's arm, trying to get the man to stop from running in front of the vehicle, but it is not working, and the man is about to not only get himself hit by the truck, but also the little girl who is attached to his hand. Hironei has never had a problem with seeing a man die, but seeing one of her sisters, one that is quite young, approaching death is something she is not going to tolerate. Hironei, not wanting the little girl to die, quickly sprouts her wings and flies her way to the man and the little girl.

The trance has the man unable to hear the horn of the truck that is about to hit him, but before anyone knows it, Hironei has come in to save the day. Before the truck can come and end the man and the little girl holding the hand of the man under Hironei's trance, Hironei has moved them and now all three of them are on the other side of the street. The man is slowly exiting the trance that Hironei accidentally put him under when she was singing her song to another man. To her knowledge, this is the first time one of her kind has saved a man.

"Are you ok?" Hironei asks the man and the little girl.

"I'm fine. Thank you, ma'am. I do wish daddy would be ok again," The little girl starts shaking her father, trying to get him out of the trance he is in.

"May I?" Hironei asks the little girl.

The little girl nods her head in agreement and Hironei begins to sing her song backwards. The trick she was taught in case any of her kind accidentally lure another sister to her death. After singing her song backwards for a few minutes, the man comes out of his trance and is sitting on the side of the street in a state of confusion.

"What happened? Where am I?" The man asks, still in confusion.

"You walked out in front of that giant monstrosity and almost hurt yourself and your little girl. It looked like something took over you," Hironei says to the man.

"Are you the one that saved me and my little Daisy?" He asks her.

"I can't say I saved you. I just know a thing or two about hypnotism." Hironei tells the man.

"Daddy, you almost walked in front of the truck and she grew wings and flew to us and saved us!" Daisy tells her father in excitement.

"I'm sorry about that, my little Daisy has an overactive imagination," the man tells Hironei, he then extends his hand, "I'm Clyde by the way, I feel I should at least shake the hand of the woman who saved me and my little Daisy from death."

Hironei was concerned that Daisy saw her wings as she flew in to save her and Clyde. Luckily for her, Clyde does not believe in mythical creatures and informs her of Daisy's overactive imagination. This makes Hironei feel relieved as she does not want anyone knowing the truth about her because it could lead to her death.

"No need for your thanks," Hironei tells Clyde, "I just didn't want to see anything happen to such a cute little girl". She then looks at Daisy and gives a smile to the cute little girl.

"You saved us. Let me do something for you in return. I insist," Clyde tells Hironei.

"You don't owe me anything," Hironei says as she begins to walk away from Clyde and Daisy. As she starts walking, Daisy asks Hironei a question.

"Can you join me and my daddy for dinner? We were going across the street to eat," Daisy tells Hironei.

Hironei, never wanting to upset another female, agrees to the offer and goes with Clyde and Daisy to the diner for food.

While Hironei has lived among humans for the last few centuries, her interaction with them has been minimal. Even though Hironei consumes food, she does not eat in restaurants where humans eat. She is looking at the menu, unable to read it, and unfamiliar with the foods that humans eat these days. Hironei looks at Daisy and asks, "What are you eating?"

"I'm getting the mac n' cheese!" Daisy tells Hironei in excitement.

"If this mac n' cheese is good enough for you then it is good enough for me too!" Hironei says in response.

Daisy starts laughing and looks at Hironei and says "The mac n' cheese is on the kid's menu. You can't have it."

"I say tonight they allow it and we eat the food of children," Hironei says as if she were about to enter a battle.

"You do know I'm paying. You can get whatever you want to eat. Uhm." Clyde says as he realizes he does not know the name of the woman he is buying dinner for, "What's your name ma'am?"

"My name is Hironei of the land Sirenum." Hironei tells Clyde. After she introduces herself, the waitress comes over, takes their orders, and the three begin talking once more while awaiting their food.

"I can't say thank you enough for saving me and my little Daisy. Thank you Hironei," Clyde says with a smile on his face as he says thank you once more to Hironei.

"I already told you, you owe me nothing. Glad to help you and this little cutie right here," Hironei says as she points to Daisy.

Clyde has never met anyone who has been as happy to see his daughter as Hironei has been. Even though he just met her, Clyde begins to think he should attempt to ask out Hironei. Before he can ask, the receipt is given to him and the diner is getting ready to close. After paying, Clyde is walking out with Hironei and Daisy. Daisy is happy and Hironei looks as if she ate at a buffet even though she barely nibbled on food from the kid's menu. Before she gets ready to leave, Clyde attempts to ask her out.

"Hironei, you saved my life, and you are such a good person to my little Daisy. I really want to see you again."

"I'm not sure if that's possible" Hironei responds as she begins to look a bit gloomy.

"Please!" Daisy says as a giant smile begins to cover her face.

"OK" Hironei says as she sees the smile upon Daisy's face, "Where do you live, and I'll visit you in the future".

"Right over there." Daisy points to a house within walking distance of the diner, "You'll know it because the house has a green door in sunlight."

"I like it! I'll visit you!" Hironei says as she smiles at both Daisy and Clyde.

After she agrees, Clyde goes to give Hironei a hug. After embracing for a few minutes, Hironei lets go and begins to walk away to the building she sits on top of while Clyde and Daisy head in the opposite direction to their house. After Clyde tucked Daisy in for bed, he went to his room and even though he had only met her, he couldn't get Hironei off his mind. She's beautiful, she's caring, and most important for him; she is very fond of his daughter, something he's had issues with in the past when he tried dating. For the first time in a while, Clyde feels he has met someone with the top quality he is looking for, someone who will treat Daisy right. He would prefer being single over dating someone that isn't good to his daughter. But Clyde knows Hironei likes Daisy, she was kind to Daisy the entire time. Given the smile on her face when Daisy pointed out where they live, he's confident he'll see her again.

The next day, Hironei keeps her promise and goes to the house with the green door. The place Daisy told her where she and her father live. Given her lack of interaction with humanity until last night, she begins to feel nervous. She feels uncertain of what to do, but before she can turn away, Clyde opens the door, and a smile comes across his face as he sees the beautiful woman who saved him the night before.

"Good afternoon Hironei!" Clyde says as he goes in for a hug. Choked, Hironei just smiles and embraces Clyde in front of his house. Even though Hironei is unsure of what will come of her time around Clyde and Daisy, she gives in. Little does she realize; those feelings Clyde has for her may be mutual.

Hironei spends the day with Clyde and Daisy. Either learning what people watch on television or just playing dolls with a child. These are things she's never done before despite being in this area for longer than Clyde has been alive. She's also learning that while she only saved Clyde because Daisy was with him, she is beginning to have feelings. Her heart speeds up, she's always smiling when he's talking to her, and she's laughing even though what he is saying isn't funny. At the end of the day, Hironei gets ready to leave. She gives Daisy a hug and as she is leaving she embraces Clyde. She buries herself into his arms. She feels safe, but she also knows who she is, or in this case, what she is. After they embrace, she leaves the house and looks for a clear area to fly back to her rooftop.

As Hironei notices no one around, she spreads her wings and flies to the top of the building where she sings her song. While she enjoyed the day with Clyde and Daisy, she couldn't help but feel that Clyde feels something for her. She even remembered she was quick to hug Clyde as she was leaving. There's several problems with this, but the main problem is she is not human. When Daisy saw the truth, Clyde chalked it up to his daughter having an overactive imagination. She isn't sure if Clyde will believe her should she tell him the truth, also, if he does believe her, will he still accept her. Would Clyde accept Hironei and let her be around his daughter? After all, her kind is known for killing. However, if she were to consummate a relationship with Clyde, she loses her abilities and her immortality. Unlike other nights when Hironei would sing her song from atop the building. Tonight, she is lost in her feelings, something she has not done in decades. Tonight, Hironei does not look down on the humans to decide which man she will sing her song to. Tonight, Hironei does not utter a tune.

Over the next few months, Hironei would visit Clyde and Daisy. At first her visits were sporadic. She would show up once every few days, she would play with Daisy then hear Clyde talk about his day and she would hang on to every word coming from his lips. She would always hug Daisy then bury herself into Clyde's arms before leaving. She knew she had feelings for Clyde and could not resist her feelings. Then, as her feelings became stronger, her visits became more frequent. At first, it was once every few days, then it became a few days a week, before Hironei noticed it, she was visiting Clyde and Daisy every day. She also noticed as she spends more time with Daisy and Clyde, the less singing she was doing at night. Hironei felt she could not lure a man to his death when she herself was soon realizing she was in love with a man.

After coming over almost every day, she noticed she was coming to visit Clyde when Daisy was in school. She came in and sat down on the sofa, next to Clyde. As they are speaking, Hironei can't help but smile as she is talking to Clyde. They speak about what Clyde is watching and after months of seeing her, Clyde decides to muster up the courage to tell Hironei how he feels about her.

"Hironei", Clyde says while trying not to clam up.

"Yes" she replies as a smile begins to cover her face.

"I…" Clyde says as he is trying to figure out the best way to tell Hironei how he feels about her, "…have feelings for you."

Hironei froze as she did not know what to do. She does have feelings for Clyde as well, she loves being around Daisy, deep down, Hironei knows that she is in love with Clyde, but she is not human and if she were to be involved romantically with Clyde, she becomes mortal. Hironei begins to sweat and starts to feel that she may panic. Afraid to tell Clyde the truth, Hironei jumps up and quickly leaves the house. She runs to an open vacant area, spreads her wings, and flies off before anyone can see her. Clyde opens the door and notices that Hironei is nowhere to be found. Now Clyde sees that the bus is stopping by to drop off Daisy. Clyde knows he needs to find Hironei and he's not sure if Daisy should join. In a decision he thinks is best, Clyde tells Daisy to go over to the neighbour's house for the moment because he needs to take care of something. Daisy makes her way to the neighbour's house as Clyde makes his way to town in hopes of finding Hironei.

Clyde goes to the place where he first met Hironei, the street near the diner. The place where she saved him and Daisy. He looks around to see if he can figure out where Hironei would be living. He looks around and isn't sure where exactly Hironei came from the night she saved him and Daisy. He then remembers Daisy telling him how Hironei had wings and flew in to save him from above. Reality soon sets within Clyde; he was saved from death by a woman who might not even be human. The crazier thing about this situation, Clyde is still in love with this woman and he wants to be with her. Clyde also feels that Hironei feels the same way about him. He then decides to go to the building down the corner from the diner. The only building in the area high enough for something as unexplainable as Daisy said to have some scope of reality.

As he is walking to the building he sees something peculiar as he looks up at the top of the building. It looks like something, or possibly someone is on the roof. Clyde goes to the door and goes inside. He looks to the left and sees the stairs that lead to the roof. He makes a beeline for the door and begins hiking the stairs to the roof.

He gets to the door and it's locked, on the inside. This proves that everything his daughter told him is true, Hironei has wings and she flew in to save the two of them from certain death. Clyde now believes everything Daisy told him about Hironei and it proves that she truly is not human. Clyde now accepts the odd truth, he is in love with an entity that is not human. Either way, he knows his feelings for Hironei are true and he begins to knock on the door, hoping to get Hironei's attention.

"Hironei, I know you're on the other side of this door. I want to talk to you. I will do whatever it takes to speak to you. I know you have the same feelings for me that I have for you. I also know that my little Daisy thinks the world of you. Either open this door or please meet me on the ground," Clyde waits a moment, he puts his ear to the door, hoping to hear Hironei coming to the door. He waits a few more minutes and he doesn't hear a thing. He knocks on the door again in hopes of Hironei opening the door for the two of them to talk. After giving it a few minutes, Clyde realizes that no one is coming to open the door. Clyde hangs his head down as he begins to go back downstairs to wait for her.

Clyde begins walking downstairs and he is wondering if he's taking his daughter's words too seriously. He is genuinely starting to believe the woman he is in love with is inhuman because his daughter said she saw a woman with wings. He is beginning to think he is crazy, but he also knows his feelings for Hironei are genuine and he wants to tell her and is willing to do whatever he possibly can to be with her. While Clyde is thinking about his daughter's words and his feelings for Hironei, he doesn't realize he is at the bottom of the stairs and accidentally runs into the door. After stumbling for a moment, Clyde realizes he is at the bottom of the stairs, takes a second to recollect himself after running into a closed door. He then opens the door and exits the area where the stairway is at. He then walks out of the building and is back on the street. Much to his surprise, once he is back outside on the street, Hironei is awaiting him outside of the building.

Clyde is uncertain if his daughter's words are true, but those words are in his head and he can't help but ask the beautiful woman in front of him. Without hesitation, Clyde cuts right to it and asks Hironei if the words Daisy told him are true.

"You were on the roof just a minute ago, right? And you didn't take the stairs, correct?" Clyde asks.

"Yes, I was, and you are correct." Hironei says as she holds her head in shame.

"Can I ask how you managed to get on a roof when the door is locked from the inside?"

Hironei steps back, holds her head down, and reveals she has a pair of wings. A pair of wings that stretch out almost eight feet, they are white, and they glow. The glow is so bright, Clyde has to shield his eyes to avoid going blind. Hironei sees that Clyde is shielding his eyes and chooses to hide her wings once more. Once Hironei hides her wings, Clyde removes his hand from covering his eyes. He sees that Hironei is feeling upset and tries his best to comfort her.

"Can I ask what you are?" Clyde says in a comforting voice, noticing Hironei seems more scared than he is at this moment.

"In the early writings of man, my sisters and I were referred to as sirens. We would sing our song from our island and lure men to their demise. After Persephone was taken from Hades, my sisters left the island. Some are still alive, many were hunted by man after their weapons became more advanced," As Hironei continues her tone becomes more emotional to the point of nearly crying, "I retreated here, I was worshipped by the natives, I was a goddess to them. Then your ancestors attacked. I was not strong enough to take them all, I went into hiding. I would sing my song to some men here and there, it is what I do and why I'm here. One night, I tried singing my song to a man only to see his ears were covered. My song must have a man to hear it, you were the closest man nearby and it lured you. I saw Daisy holding your hand and I can never let a sister die, and I saved the two of you. Saving you and Daisy was the first time I truly saved a man," Hironei tells Clyde as she has her head down.

"You mean to tell me, you are the reason why I almost was hit by a truck and you then saved me?" Clyde asks

"Yes, my song needed a man to lure and you were the first one to hear my song." Hironei says as she holds her head in shame.

"I think it means you and I were meant to be. I am the first man you saved, regardless of the circumstances."

"Clyde, I am a siren." Hironei says to Clyde, "My sole purpose on this planet is to kill men, we become mortal if we consummate with a man. Becoming mortal is a punishment for sirens."

Clyde hearing Hironei tell him she is a siren makes him feel the conversation needs to be lightened. "I thought sirens were mermaids, not birds," Clyde says trying to make the conversation less heavy-hearted.

"It's a complicated story. I know you love me, but I'm not human. If you and I were to consummate our relationship, I lose my wings, my song, and I become mortal."

"If you become mortal, you and I can be together. You sound like you have had too many hardships. You, me, and Daisy can have a fairy-tale ending." Clyde says as he tries to move in on Hironei and puts his hand upon her face.

Hironei holds his hand as it touches her face. She knows she loves Clyde as much as he loves her. She wants to be a part of Daisy's life as well. Clyde mentioning her hardships of being an immortal are more truthful than he knows. However, Hironei is still uncertain if this could ever work. She looks up at Clyde and begins singing. While Clyde is in a trance, she flies him back to his house. As Clyde is still in a trance, she sings her song backwards, the same thing she did when she first met him, to get him out of the trance. She then quickly leaves before Daisy returns home because she knows seeing Daisy at this moment will put her in tears. She also knows it will make Daisy cry as well.

As Clyde is regaining consciousness, Daisy comes running into the house thinking she saw Hironei. She sees her father and he's in the same condition from the night he almost got himself and Daisy ran over.

"Daddy!" Daisy says as she is shaking her father. "What's wrong?"

"Huh!?" Clyde says as he realizes what happened. "Sorry Daisy. Everything is ok. You can let me go now sweetie."

"Ok. Is Hironei here?"

"I don't think we'll be seeing Hironei anymore."

"What happened?"

"You remember when you told me about how she flew in to save us?" Clyde asks Daisy. Daisy nods her head. Then, Clyde continues to speak. "Well, she said because of her wings she doesn't know if she can be around us anymore. She told me being around us could hurt us."

As Clyde is saying this, Daisy begins to cry. There hasn't been anyone in her life besides her father. For the first time she has met someone who makes her dad happy and someone she enjoys being around. Daisy tells her dad she is going with him this time to talk to Hironei and she will be coming back with them. She walks inside and makes her way over to the coat rack by the door, grabs her coat, her gloves, and her father's coat. She then opens the door and hands her father his coat. She tells her father in a demanding tone to take her to Hironei. Even though she is a little kid, Clyde does exactly as Daisy says and the two make their way to the building.

The two make their way to the building and Clyde once again calls for Hironei. He mentions Daisy is with him and to at least say goodbye to Daisy if she isn't going to be around anymore. The two stand there and wait for Hironei to fly down to them. As they are looking up, Hironei walks from the side of the building to where they are standing.

"Clyde? Daisy?" Hironei says in a soft voice as she is afraid to startle them while they are looking up.

Daisy runs to Hironei and gives her a hug and begins speaking to her. "You need to come home with us. Daddy loves you and you love daddy! We don't care about your wings. We want you in our family."

Hironei, while wrapping her arms around the small child, tells her, "If your daddy and I become a family, I lose my wings. I'll just be a normal human. That means if you tell anyone about my wings, I'll be unable to show them my wings because I won't have them anymore."

"I don't care. I love you Hironei," Daisy responds to Hironei as she is being held by Clyde, she removes herself from Clyde's grip and goes over to Hironei and hugs her. Clyde then walks over and the three of them begin hugging. Hironei lets go of Daisy for a moment and the second she lets go, Clyde does not hesitate this time like he did when they were at his house, he decides to move in and kisses Hironei. At first Hironei is shocked that Clyde would move in so fast. Then she gives in, her eyes close and she wraps her arms around Clyde. She moves in closer and embraces the kiss a little longer. After they kiss, Hironei looks lovingly into Clyde's eyes, she takes his hand and puts it on her face. She then wraps his arms around her and puts her head into his chest as he holds her. She looks into Clyde's eyes and moves in to kiss him once more. She then puts her head on Clyde's chest, knowing what she is about to ask him is something she knows will change her life. While Clyde is holding Hironei, she asks him one question, "Can we go home?".

"YES!" Daisy excitedly responds to Hironei before Clyde can even give a response. Daisy's excitement of Hironei becoming a part of their family puts a smile on Hironei's face. Clyde sees the excitement on Daisy's face, the happiness Hironei shows when she is around Daisy and that moment is when Clyde knows the woman he is in love with is the perfect woman for him. He doesn't care that she's beautiful, he doesn't care that she isn't human. Hironei loves Daisy and Daisy loves Hironei and that is all that Clyde has ever wanted in a woman, someone that will love his daughter and be good to her. Clyde grabs Daisy's hand with one arm and wraps his vacant arm around his true love, Hironei. He smiles and the three of them begin their journey home.

Clyde is walking home with a smile on his face. He has his daughter to one side of him and the first woman he's loved in quite some time on the other. At this moment, Clyde feels like his life is perfect. He has everything he could ever want in life and knows that asking for more would be greedy on his behalf. The three of them head home and begin their life as a family.

***

Hironei and Clyde eventually get married and Hironei adopts Daisy as her own daughter. She eventually consummates her relationship with Clyde, even though she loses her wings, her song, and her immortality, she discovers that Clyde was right, and her hardships were soon gone as she now has a family and for the first time in her life, she has happiness. She never knew how much misery she had in her life until she met Clyde and Daisy. Her life was spent killing men and the moment she chose to save a man, it brought happiness into her life.

22

RED ON BLACK

by J. Jerome

The sound of straw sandals running across the polished wooden floor broke the still silence of the early morning. He seemed to be running away from the crawling light of the sun as it inched slowly upwards from the east. A few minutes later, the man was stopped by the outstretched hand of an armed guard wearing full armour made from wooden plates and red laces.

"The Shogun is having breakfast. He cannot be interrupted," the guard declared immediately when the runner was within hearing range.

"I have an urgent message for the Shogun. It cannot wait," he replied while trying to catch his breath

"You know he'll have your head if your message is not worth the interruption, Shino!" the guard insisted.

"I know, Hidetsuge. But believe me, he'll have both our heads if he doesn't hear this one right away," Shino insisted. His breathing has become calmer, relaxed. He stared straight into Hidetsuge's eyes to prove to him that he was serious.

"Very well," Hidetsuge said as he shifted from his position and grabbed the wooden handle of the door and pulled it gently. The door opened silently, it's finely carved frame a worthy introduction to the splendour of the room within. "You may enter at your own peril," he whispered with caution. He doesn't want to risk the Shogun hearing what he said to Shino.

"Yes? What is it?" the Shogun asked with a scowl when he heard the door to his private chamber open.

Shino immediately took two steps into the chamber then immediately dropped down until his forehead touched the back of his hands while his palm was flat on the floor. The sound of the chamber door closing was Shino's signal to speak. "I apologize for the intrusion, my lord, but I have very urgent news. The Black Ronin has returned!" Shino said without raising his head from the floor.

"What?!" the Shogun exclaimed as he threw down his chopsticks on the table. "Are you sure of this? Answer me now or I'll have your head!" the Shogun roared at the shaking Shino who had not moved from his spot.

"I am sure of it my lord. All the farmers that have brought in their goods from the villages of Sionan and Redwood say the same thing!" Shino reported.

"Sionan and Redwood? Villages that are bordered by the mountain ranges. He's clever to have chosen to pass that way in order to avoid the border patrols. These villages are at least a day away from here by a cart, are they not?" the Shogun asked. He has obviously calmed down and looked like he was in deep thought.

"Yes, they are, my lord," Shino replied.

"So, these farmers that have reported this, they're the only ones who survived?" the Shogun asked. His voice sounded concerned and his scowl had faded a little.

"What do you mean, my lord?" Shino asked uneasily. He was sure that he'd be punished for not understanding what the Shogun meant. He wasted the Shogun's time by making him repeat himself.

However, the Shogun's anger at getting his breakfast interrupted seemed to have completely faded away. He understood why Shino risked the intrusion to bring him the urgent news. And urgent it was indeed. "These farmers that reported the Black Ronin's arrival; were they the only ones who survived his attack? Did he burn their entire village?" the Shogun explained patiently.

"It was nothing like that, my lord. He did not kill anyone nor burn or damage any property when he passed these two villages," Shino replied.

"Are you sure? He did nothing? He just passed through those villages?" the Shogun roared once again in complete surprise.

"I am sure of it, my lord. I asked them specifically if they needed your lordship's assistance; medical or otherwise. But they all said the same thing; no one was injured, and nothing was destroyed. He merely went into an inn for bread and tea that he paid for and left," Shino narrated hurriedly but clearly.

***

"If he passed by Sionan and Redwood two days ago and never stopped there, he'd likely arrive at the gates of the city by sunrise tomorrow," a middle-aged man who wore a cyan-coloured silk kimono said as he pointed at an area on the large map in front of him and his companions.

"We must also consider the possibility that he will be entering the capital via a route that is not obvious. And since he entered via Sionan, this means that he wanted to avoid attention as much as possible. At least until he has accomplished whatever it is that he aims to do," said another middle-aged man in white kimono with golden trimmings.

"I agree with Hiroshi. He will keep himself hidden until he is ready to do his diabolical plan. And I have a good idea of what that plan is!" a young man exclaimed then slammed his fist on the large wooden table where the map rested. He wore a sky-blue silken kimono embroidered with cranes.

"What do you think is he planning to do, Mitzuo?" Hiroshi asked as he turned to the young man in crane kimono.

He took a deep breath as his face hardened. "He's here to harass the Shogun's daughter, Reiko. He knows that our wedding is on the next full moon. He will not allow that to happen!" Mitzuo replied with bitterness and anger in his voice. Hiroshi nodded in agreement but said nothing.

"Yes, it only makes sense," the man in cyan kimono said softly.

"He was banished exactly six winters ago, on the same full moon of our upcoming wedding. This is symbolic for him, Takahiro," Mitzuo added.

"They say the number six is the number of love. Maybe it is true because six winters ago he was rejected by Reiko. Thus, love was lost and was turned into hate that caused him to go berserk and kill an unarmed man," a silent old man in one corner explained patiently. "At the same time, it was also six winters ago that Reiko accepted Mitzuo. The return of Kazuo the Black Ronin is not just a plan. It is destiny."

"It is...destiny, Sensei Sora?" Mitzuo asked in disbelief.

"Yes. You grew up together. I trained you both, you served the same lord, and you both loved the same girl. You are like the sun and the moon. Darkness and the light. You must face him before you can marry Reiko, or your marriage will never know peace. Now come, Mitzuo, I will teach you something that might help you when you face him. You two were always too evenly matched. This little something might help turn the duel slightly to your favour."

***

"Mother, why do people fear the Black Ronin?"

"Because he killed an unarmed man in cold blood when Reiko turned down his proposal. And he's been raiding and pillaging villages south of Heaven's Gate ever since."

"Is he called the Black Ronin because he wears a black kimono with a red circle on the back?"

"It's a blood moon, my son. They say that the full moon was red when he killed that man. Wait, where did you hear about all that?"

"A man wearing a red full moon on a black kimono just passed by, mom."

"What? He's here? How did he get into the capital? I just saw several samurais on horseback headed for the city gate this morning."

"He doesn't look like a bad man, mom. His face looks calm."

"What are you talking about? Get away from there and close all the windows and lock the door quickly!"

***

"General Hiroshi, I have a report from the city gate where the ten samurais were dispatched."

"Good. They should be settled there already. It's almost nightfall."

"T-That is what my report is about, sir."

"Okay, that'll be all. Dismissed."

"Uh, sir. They're all dead."

"What?!"

"The Black Ronin killed them all when they tried to stop him from entering the city gate!"

"He killed all ten samurais on horseback?"

"Yes, sir. And the exact words of the wall guards were; 'killed them without much effort, men and horses, both'."

"So, he's here already. And he dared pass through the main gate of the city. When was this?"

"Just this afternoon sir."

***

The city was immediately placed on high alert. Guards in groups of five patrolled the streets. They were all issued a whistle in case they encountered the Black Ronin. The whistle would alert the other groups and the samurais that guard the palace of the Shogun. Despite the quiet of the evening, no one within the vicinity of the palace was able to sleep well. They all anticipated an attack.

"I can't believe it! He cut down all ten of them!"

"I was in training with two of those men."

"They had three advantages against him, and he still defeated them. Speed of the horse, high ground since they're on horseback and the numbers!"

"And I needed only one advantage to defeat them. Years of experience killing samurai."

The two samurai turned around with weapons drawn to look at the person whose voice had interrupted their conversation. A samurai wearing a black satin kimono faced them with a grin on his face and both arms crossed in front of him. The two samurai immediately jumped into a battle stance and prepared to engage the stranger.

"I defeated ten samurai on horseback quite easily. There's only two of you on foot. Your odds don't look too good."

"We have sworn to protect the Shogun!"

"I'm not here to bring harm to the Shogun nor to his daughter. You can rest easy that I will hurt no one until the sun rises," Kazuo said in the same deep voice. He then slowly lowered his head and stared at the two samurai with a steely gaze. "Unless I am forced to defend myself."

"I-If the Shogun is not in danger then we are not really needed here."

"Yes. We'd better go where we're needed!"

The two samurais sheathed their swords and hurriedly walked away.

***

Tagawa Mitzuo had always been a light sleeper. Even though he barely slept that evening, his senses were suddenly on high alert. He got up from his bed and looked around inside his plainly decorated room. There was no one inside the room but him. His windows were closed exactly how he left them before he slept. He found nothing out of the ordinary and was about to go back to sleep when he jumped out of bed once more. There, on top of the dresser was a plain sheet of linen paper.

'Meet me at the city square. Sunrise. Fail to appear and I will burn down the capital. – TBR'.

***

A small crowd has gathered around the city plaza. They were watching the man in black kimono who sat motionless in front of the fountain on the western side. The rays of the sun had started to light up the small beads of water at the top of the fountain when a large group of men on horseback arrived at the eastern side of the plaza.

The Shogun, the generals of the army and of the police were there. A retinue of samurai, Sensei Sora and Reiko were with them. The sight of Reiko getting off her horse finally stirred the motionless Black Ronin.

"You will surrender yourself immediately," the Shogun started to say but was rudely interrupted.

"Silence! I do not answer to you anymore. You lost that privilege a long time ago," Kazuo said angrily.

"What do you want?" Mitzuo asked as he stepped forward.

"A duel. The winner takes Reiko home."

"She is not mine to give."

"It doesn't matter. No one will be able to stop me from doing so once you're dead. I will take your life away before the end of the duel," Kazuo replied in a deep voice. Reiko shuddered in fear. This was not the same Kazuo that she knew. His very voice struck fear in the heart of the people that have gathered to watch the duel.

"Then I will have to stop you permanently," Mitzuo replied with grim determination. His sharp eyes immediately noticed that Kazuo had a katana on his left side and another on his back.

"It is decided then! Sensei Sora, announce the rules of the duel before we formally start!" Kazuo called out as he stood from where he was sitting. He stepped forward slowly opposite Mitzuo.

"This is a duel of honour. No one may join in the battle favouring either side. None of the combatants is allowed to accept any form of assistance under penalty of dishonour. The combatants cannot strike an unarmed opponent under penalty of banishment and dishonour! This duel will not end until one of you dies or have surrendered in shame. If you both agree to these terms, then let the duel begin!" Sensei Sora announced loudly then immediately stepped back after he finished speaking.

Mitzuo jumped forward right away and started to circle Kazuo. He initially planned to play defensive in order to gauge Kazuo's skill, but his anger got the best of him. He immediately lunged forward and used a powerful slice from the lower left side that was too fast for most of the people present to see. A loud metallic ringing sound filled the air as Mitzuo's katana was deftly blocked by the katana at Kazuo's side. Kazuo immediately threw a counterattack by slashing downward with the katana on his back. Mitzuo jumped back and barely avoided getting hit by the deadly blow.

'So, that's what the katana on his side is for!' Mitzuo thought.

Mitzuo was not discouraged and went for another attack. He moved forward fast with a feint and did a quick partial pirouette and slashed sideways at Kazuo, but the same defensive tactic was there to foil his attack. Mitzuo did a number of relentless attacks that combined multiple feints and slashes from different directions, but Kazuo was always ready to defend against them while his counterattacks steadily gained speed.

'You can do it Mitzuo. You can't let him win!' Reiko thought to herself.

'Kazuo's speed has greatly increased! If Mitzuo doesn't break through his defence soon, he will tire out and become helpless once Kazuo makes his attack!' Sensei Sora thought.

'I can't get through his defence! He's barely moving while I'm slowly tiring out! He has not even made a direct attack! I have to use the secret technique! But if it fails, I am done for!'

Mitzuo decided that the battle would become a disadvantage to him if it lasted longer. He made a move towards the left and did a double feint and then executed the manoeuvre. He pivoted on his right foot and made a full pirouette drawing both his katana and koshirae.

Kazuo ran forward towards Mitzuo to meet his new attack!

The spinning slash came from the right. The side where Kazuo had a harder time defending from. When the spin was complete, Mitzuo's katana completely missed Kazuo, but he did not slow down. He continued the full spin, and he felt his koshirae connect. His hand felt the vibration of broken ribs, as well as the koshirae, cracking under the intensity of the attack.

Mitzuo then used the counter momentum of the impact to reverse his spin and lunge his katana into Kazuo's chest. He finally opened his eyes and saw the grinning face of Kazuo merely inches away from his. Mitzuo twisted his katana and lunged it deeper into Kazuo's chest as he screamed out all of his anger.

"Mitzuo!" Sensei Sora exclaimed.

But Mitzuo wanted to bask in his victory and lunged his katana deeper once again and then kicked Kazuo away as he pulled his katana out. Just as Kazuo fell to the ground, Mitzuo suddenly noticed that Kazuo's twin katana were almost six feet away from where he fell. His eyes immediately looked at the fallen body of Kazuo and saw that he was completely weaponless.

"Didn't I tell you..." Kazuo coughed out blood as he spoke. "I will take your life away before the duel is over...Mitzuo the Ronin."

Mitzuo's eyes shook as tears fell from them until all he could see was the flowing red on black.

23

TRAMPLED

by Manoj Vaz

Ajit Koshy could see his hands shivering. He was also getting an unbearable ache in his joints. It was afternoon and he hadn't had his smoke yet. Ajit was addicted to brown sugar and he knew he had to get down to the local dealer to get his 'package'.

But today, he was excited and confused. He had caught something on his camera that could fetch him a lot of money, but it could also be very dangerous.

Ajit was the 24-year-old son of Antony 'Tony' Koshy, the reputed wildlife photographer of the seventies and eighties. Tony Koshy's magical reproduction of the Asiatic lions of Gir forest, the Royal Bengal tigers of Ranthambore and the Elephants of Nilgiris were still considered as the best reproductions of Indian wildlife by any photographer.

Then while on a trip to shoot African elephants in Kenya, he got too close to a herd and was attacked and trampled by a protective female.

After three months in a hospital in Nairobi, he came back to India on a wheelchair, a paraplegic, paralyzed from the waist down.

And incredibly fortuitous to be alive. After all, very few survive an elephant attack.

Ajit was only 14 then and they lived in a big apartment overlooking the sea in Shivaji Park, an up-market area in Central Bombay.

Post his injury, his friends and colleagues quietly disappeared, and Tony took his ire out on his wife Shirley and Ajit.

Unable to bear him, Shirley left him for his best friend or rather his ex-best friend whose only condition was that she should come alone.

That left Ajit at the mercy of his bedridden, cynical father and he never forgave his mother for abandoning him at that formative juncture of his life.

Tony needed a full-time nurse and someone to take care of Ajit. The doctor treating him arranged for a nurse and Tony recruited an ex-assistant of his named Michael to look after Ajit.

Medium height, dark, wiry, and mean, Michael moved in with the Koshys and soon was humping the ugly nurse in the day and sodomizing Ajit at night.

Michael was addicted to hashish and brown sugar and he got young Ajit addicted too.

Tony passed away in 1995 leaving behind huge debts. Ajit had to sell their swanky apartment to repay the debts and got himself a small one-bedroom apartment just outside city limits in Dahisar.

He got rid of Michael and the nurse and lived alone. The locality was shady and surrounded by pick up joints and 'rent by the hour' lodges.

The area suited Ajit because it was easy to get his daily dose of brown sugar without much fuss.

His father's Nikon SLR with telescopic lenses was the only inheritance he had left. With no source of income and an expensive addiction, Ajit hit upon a novel idea for subsistence.

From his bedroom window, he could see the rooms of Night Palace Lodge which was across the road. He would train his camera into the rooms, with the powerful telescopic zoom catching details that were beyond natural eyesight.

Every other day, he would catch a drunk, married man with a prostitute in the room on his camera, before the lights were switched off.

Ajit had an accomplice who worked at the reception of the lodge. He would provide him with the contact details of the man from the hotel register.

Ajit would then approach the man and offer to sell the photos and negatives to him for a small cost. He was careful not to be too greedy and conducted his blackmailing with a great deal of honesty. He would ask for Rs. 5000 and if the victim haggled, he would settle for Rs. 3000.

This way, the victim would not feel the pinch and avoid going to the cops. After all, the victim knew that the cops would extort a lot more than Rs. 5000 if he went to them.

But last night his drug-infused sleep was disturbed with a nightmare of an elephant chasing him down and trampling him.

Ajit had woken up with a start, his heart palpitating and sweating profusely.

He had peed a little in his pyjamas, so he had gotten up to empty his bladder and change into dry shorts. Since he was too scared to go back to sleep, he went to the window to peer outside.

Through his sleepy eyes, he could see a shadowy figure climbing the drainage pipeline of the hotel from the outside.

Ajit immediately took out his camera and started clicking. He could see the man get on to the veranda of Room 109 on the first floor and knock on the glass of the French windows.

Soon the light to the room was switched on and a pretty girl, who looked like a high-class call girl opened the veranda door and let him in.

They seemed to be arguing over something. After a couple of minutes, the light was switched off. Fifteen minutes later he saw the man leave the same way as he had come in and get into a car and drive away.

Ajit was a little confused. His telescopic lenses had clearly caught the man. He had seen that he was wearing leather gloves that bikers wear. But he had come in a car.

It all seemed very fishy to Ajit. He couldn't sleep at first but dozed off later only to be woken up by the sound of thunder. It was dawn and raining heavily. When he went to the window, he could see a police van parked outside the lodge.

He immediately called his accomplice from the lodge and found out about the murder. A bead of sweat trickled down behind his ear.

His initial reaction was that he had stumbled upon a jackpot. But then, it was a case of murder, suddenly a chill ran up his spine.

Blackmailing a murderer could be extremely life-threatening. After all, every murderer knew that the punishment for one murder and multiple murders was the same under the law.

He immediately dismantled his camera and hid it in a trunk under his bed. He knew that the right thing to do was to go to the police. But the cops being cops would dig into his modus operandi and would book him for blackmailing instead of being thankful.

'No cops,' he thought, 'I have to lay low for a few days.' He was shivering and it was not just because he had not had his fix yet.

All of next week, he could see cops coming and going out of the lodge. Ajit would get daily reports about the progress of the investigation from his friend. He was so scared that he did not even tell his accomplice that he had captured the murderer on camera, but he had a feeling that given his interest in the case, he knew.

Finally, he decided to destroy the roll. Just then the doorbell rang.

'Who could that be?' wondered Ajit, he hardly had any visitors.

He gingerly opened the door.

A stocky, middle-aged, nondescript man with a pencil-thin moustache and oily hair stood in front of him, smiling amicably.

"Hello Ajit, I am Ram Shastri, your friend and your greatest well-wisher!"

And before his drug dazed eyes could focus, Ram Shastri had already wedged his foot in the door and pushed himself inside.

"I believe you have something that is of interest to me. Don't worry; I am willing to pay you well for it." Shastri waved a thick wad of 100-rupee notes at him.

"Err... no... nothing... what do you mean?" Ajit was flustered and distracted by the wad of notes swaying in front of him. He was broke and turkeying.

"Be a good boy and hand over the roll to me and you can forget that I was ever here," continued Shastri cheerfully.

"How did you k..k..know? Are you a c..cop?" Ajit was ready to faint.

"The police are dumb. They know nothing and they need not know anything," came the reply, "Come on son, you don't want me to report you to the police, do you?"

Shastri was still smiling but a chill went up Ajit's spine. There was something very scary and real about the man.

Ajit immediately took out the film from the camera and gave it to him. Shastri smiled again and threw the wad of notes at him and patted him on his back.

"Good boy… now you can forget I was here."

By the time Ajit bent down to pick up the money and looked up, he had vanished. Ajit closed the door. He was sweating profusely. He was never so scared in his life. He was sure the man would have shot him dead for the film roll if he had refused to comply.

For the second time in the week, he found that he had wet his pants.

24

UNFORTUNATE

by Debajit Deb

Waaji City, 2020

The crime rate crossed the highest recorded limit. Corruption rampaged in every field. People lived in terror. If there could be a place as an epitome of misery and hopelessness, it was the Waaji City, suffocating under Adnan, an underworld kingpin. He was the uncrowned ruler of the city. He brought justice, law, and peace to their knees.

No one was there to question him. If anyone dared to raise their voice against him, their entire family used to pay with their lives. Adnan's minions utilized his power and did whatever they wanted; even the police couldn't do anything to him.

There was a day, one day when Adnan's rule was challenged. And that was a prolix story.

2010

Rana Dev Shukla, the renowned officer who had an immensely heroic track record was transferred to the city. He had never let any malefactor reign anywhere he was transferred. He joined the Waaji

City Police as DGP officer. He shifted to the city with his wife Jaya and a little boy, Rajan.

On the very first day when Rana was on the way to his office, his eyes met with the sight of a group of teenage boys assaulting a girl. The girl was asking passers-by for help. Shockingly, some of the nearby stalls quickly shut down their shutters on seeing this.

Rana expeditiously halted his car and peregrinated to her avail; he slapped those boys and took them to the station and locked them up.

"They're Adnan's minions!", a constable had pleaded with him not to apprehend those criminals.

"Adnan who??"

 The man was spellbound. "The sun sets here only by Adnan's orders."

"Not anymore !"

Rana was valiant and determined by nature. He verbalized that he was there to perform his obligation to the country and make the city malefaction free. So, he ignored any admonishments and went on to round up all the malefactors from all around the city.

Rana paid no heed as he was not trepidatious of anyone. Not long after, he ceased the operation of some of Adnan's illegal distilleries on his very first day.

The next day, as he was seated on the table a few men had strolled into the station. They got comfortable on the seats. They endeavoured to admonish him and to take back the locked boys stating or rather blowing the trumpets of Adnan.

But Rana refused to budge. "The FIR has already been filed. The boys shall be produced in the court and from there, to wherever the court decides."

He called out to the receding goons, who did so only after a little bit of persuasion, "Tell your Adnan to come to the station and then we will discuss releasing the boys."

They went back, shooting daggers at him. "You're making an immensely colossal mistake! You'll regret this..", they had warned as they left the station. Threats weren't something incipient to Rana. He chuckled to himself and perpetuated his work.

That day in the evening when Rana reached home he noticed that a car had been parked by the gate. He entered and found four or five men surrounding the living room and someone sitting on his sofa. His wife was sitting on the other side, her face was drenched with fear.

Sensing trouble, Rana endeavoured to take his revolver. Suddenly, the sitting man stood up and smiled widely at Rana.

"Hello Rana sir, I am Adnan. You would have heard of me, haven't you?" He gestured to the sofa, signing Rana to sit down.

Rana stood there with clenched teeth.

"Sorry sir, you had asked me to come to the police station, but I couldn't. So, I cerebrated to pay you a visit in your house. And so here I am".

Giving nothing away, Rana glanced around the room for Rajan, mitigated that he was not there.

Rana described the gun in Adnan's hand then.

"Are you not happy, sir?" "I thought you would be jubilant to see me... Hmm .. okay, and no worries. I'll stop beating about the bush. The thing is that I don't need any trouble in my life.. and because of that for all these years I have been ruling here placidly, no one had raised any finger against me. So, why should I give myself any trouble with you who raised their voice against me? Please do cooperate with me and sit with her".

Rana ambulated up to the sofa and sat mutely. Jaya was crying and imploring Adnan not to kill them and that they will leave the city. Adnan replied, "Sorry Bhabhi Ji, it's about my reputation in Waaji" and shot both of them down. They paid no attention to the other rooms of the house or the boy peeping through the windowpanes of his room.

After Adnan left, Rajan emerged from his room upstairs. He cried bitterly and endeavoured to wake them up, but they were long gone. After some time, a few neighbours had come and aided young Rajan to do the last rites for his parents. Though a witness, Rajan could do nothing to bring justice to his murdered parents. Rajan had gone straight to the police station and told them that he had seen Adnan kill his family and beseeched them to help him.

No one paid any attention to him. Disheartened, as he was about to depart, an elderly officer had pulled him aside and told him everything about Adnan and how the system works in his favours. Disillusioned and backstabbed by the very system his father fought for, he longed for revenge.

From then on, disfigured and mutilated bodied of men known to be Adnan's minions began to be found from around the city. He was unstoppable. Whenever he chanced upon any of Adnan's boys alone, he killed them so brutally that no one could even identify whose body it was. He took care that no trace led to him.

Years went by as he prepared himself. He knew his time shall come.

2020

Adnan joined politics, clean of his past misdeeds. He had handed over the keys to his black deeds to his brother Izan, merely a puppet in his hands. It was a secret known to everyone that it was Adnan behind Izan. The city choked under them.

The crime rate crossed the highest recorded limit. Corruption rampaged in every field. People lived in terror. If there could be a place as an epitome of misery and hopelessness, it was the Waaji City, suffocating under Adnan, the underworld kingpin. He was the uncrowned ruler of the city. He brought justice, law, and peace to their knees.

He continued the murders. Anyone who was found to support Adnan or Izan paid with their lives. It was a deadly game he played.

When it was the right time, after he had killed a few of Adnan's boys, he spun a tale to the rest that there was a psycho killer in the city who had his eyes set on Adnan.

The next step, to become one with the herd, he confessed to have seen the killer and that he could recognise him. He was taken, as quickly as possible, to Izan.

Armed with a gun, given to him by Izan himself, who had told him, "if you happen to see the killer anywhere, haul him to me if not, unload all these bullets into his head."

Like a wolf, he gained the trust of Izan, waiting for his chance, his revenge, Adnan. Stealthily, he finished them off, one by one. He hadn't met Adnan yet. He was waiting, the beast in him prowling.

And very soon he had it.

A few days later Izan told Rajan that Adnan's daughter was coming home and gave him the responsibility to bring her home safely. He jumped at his chance and grabbed it, his door to Adnan.

He picked her up and drove straight to his lair instead of Adnan's place. Nidhi. That was her name. She was pretty, with an angelic soul, nothing like her father. She was born and spent her childhood in other countries with her mother. She was in Waaji for the first time ever, and that was to meet her father for the first time.

But the day she reached Waaji, he had abducted her. He knew he was playing a cat and mouse game with Adnan.

Adnan screeched at his minions to find Nidhi somehow; otherwise, he shall burn the city. He threatened them all, casting away the reputation he had built in his political field.

Izan had tasted Rajan's betrayal by then, bitter in his mouth. Word reached Adnan, who hurled his threats, scattering them aimlessly at Rajan. Rajan simply asked Izan to come and to get her. She was but a pawn.

Maddened by power and rage, Izan and his boys marched to his place but in vain. They all ended up victims of Rajan's unquenched revenge.

With a little bit of compassion still dwelling in, he asked Nidhi not to do anything that could make him kill her as his only revenge was with her father who had caused the deaths of countless innocents again and again where he had lost his family.

"Then why do you have me here? Go to my father and kill him for all I care. Let me go!".

"I don't just want to kill him. I want him to feel the pain he had given me before; I want to see the fear in his eyes. Soon, I shall have it. So, keep quiet until then. I will leave you, you are just a bait, a pawn.."

The next morning before the sun rose, he drove, with her still in captivity, out of the city. He pulled over to the cremation grounds, and to see the corner where his parents were buried. He wanted to tell them how close he was in avenging their deaths.

The return to the city was made carefully, with her strangely quiet. She had her share of questions for him once they reached his lair. After all, she had known the kind of life her father lead, Rajan was only one of the unfortunate ones who had everything snatched away by her father.

He had nothing to tell her, as she continued her story. Though born to Adnan, she had never known him, even for a moment. Her mother had not wanted anything to do with him- she had crossed the seas and left the country to put some distance between them so that even his shadow did not fall over them.

She held Rajan's hand as she reassured him. He saw in her eyes how he had let himself become after his mother's death. He saw how Adnan had ruined not just one, but countless innocent lives. He felt a tug in his heart as he let the words out. He saw his mother's face in her, warm and loving. He told her his story and how he got where he was.

How no one was there to help him, and he fought alone, and it pawned his childhood, his youth, his all happiness, with nothing to reap. Nothing he does is going to give him back what he had lost.

As he spoke, his eyes were no more able to carry the pain and were flooded with tears, she hugged him tightly. It felt to him that it was the safest place on the earth which he was wondering about for many years, and maybe it is the place where he can spend the rest of his life, a home he could never have. As he held her for a moment, savouring the peace, the sudden deafening roar of a gun reached his ears followed by Nidhi drawing in a long breath. Her hands loosened around him as she slowly crumpled to the ground. He looked to his front and saw Adnan pointing the gun towards them and another bullet came, piercing Nidhi's body with a jolt.

Rajan stood stunned, it was like the same moment when Adnan slaughtered his father and mother. He slowly landed her body to his knee and looked into her eyes, which glistened with unshed tears. She tried to say something but wasn't able to complete her words. A drop of tear appeared in his eyes and dropped onto her forehead, even though he had nothing with her.

He felt loss, burning through his veins as it dawned on him that he was the reason for her death. Adnan came close to them and looked at his daughter. "I am sorry my child, but he is my enemy, and he destroyed my army, my unmarred political image. And you were hugging him... So, I don't have any other options now.."

He lay her down and ran towards Adnan, like a hurricane in motion. No one could bear the rage he had built up. He destroyed everyone in his path. At last, he stood, bloodied, chest heaving and yet the fire of vengeance still burning brighter than ever.

Adnan began to back off, only to be dragged along, a while later with bones broken and his white overalls blotched with blood.

A while later, Adnan stood swaying on his knees, the gun pointed at his forehead. Fear danced in his eyes. He incoherently mumbled, begging to be spared.

The gun was shot thrice, two of which were found in Adnan's chest, while a single bullet was found lodged in Rajan's skull.

25

HEARTACHE

by Snehal Agarwal

He tossed and turned in his bed in the middle of the night, feeling a myriad of emotions rise in the pit of his stomach. He kept reminding himself, "Tomorrow is a big day Dhruv, you need to rest!" However, the train of his thoughts was not coming to a halt anytime soon.

He moved around in his bed to find a comfortable position, adjusted his pillows, and tugged the blankets tighter around himself, with no luck. He just couldn't sleep. His body ached from all the rushing he had been doing since a while for the upcoming event and demanded some rest, but his mind refused to calm down.

Every time he closed his eyes, Sara's beautiful face flashed in front of him. Her long, silky hair falling on her face, as her innocence filled eyes stared at him with hope. Days when they would spend sunny afternoons together, his hand caressing her hair as she lay in his lap while watching their favourite shows, popped up in his mind.

Her smile had always made his heart skip a beat and those rosy cheeks, tempted him to pull them softly. He chuckled as he imagined the weird faces she would make to tease him and how she would stick her tongue out every time she proved her point to him anytime they argued.

 He remembered how she used to repeat his name again and again until he gave up on what he was doing and gave her attention. She always said, "I simply love saying your name." Dhruv had always wondered why and how anyone would love to say someone's name but now his ears longed to hear her voice calling for him, just for one last time.

He trembled as the beautiful memories turned to the night she called his name for the last time, her voice cracking, almost on the verge of crying. Her nails had dug deep into his arms as she held him tightly, refusing to let go. Controlling his emotions, he had ignored her pleas and freed his hand from her grasp. Her swollen and teary eyes stabbed him in his gut yet could not stop him from leaving her.

He shook his head, trying to shake away the thoughts. He only wanted to cherish the good days. Her laughter echoed in his ears and the memorable times they had spent together occupied his mind. Their secret rendezvous after office hours or their random plans to eat at some small, cozy place, played in his mind on repeat. He recalled how Sara used to text him just to tell him how much she missed him. The days when she would stand outside his office or surprise him at the metro station. He knew he couldn't ever forget them. He even missed the short cab-rides which usually lead them to spend more time together.

He revelled in the memories until her screams and sobs engulfed him. She had begged him for an explanation; but he had turned away, without a second glance. He had abandoned her, the woman who loved him with all her heart and soul. "I wish I could erase that day from our memories!" he sighed as his eyes moistened.

He felt a tingle in his palm on reminiscing the night he held her hand for the first time. It was late evening, and they were walking on the streets along with their common friends. Dhruv was walking a little ahead with a few boys and she was strolling behind with another friend. A small smile played on his lips as he remembered Sara shouting, "Dhruv I can't cross this road alone, come here!" when all of us had crossed the street easily.

He had come back running to her as she was acting like a little baby. While guiding her to cross the busy road, he had clutched her hand so tightly, never wanting to let it go. Their hands had fit like the pieces of a puzzle that was meant to be. His cheeks had turned deep red thinking about how Sara would react to him holding her hand. However, she had pressed his hand softly and looked at him with pure happiness. That's when he had realised that she was the one.

Now, this realisation was just another dream that would haunt him every night. He could only imagine the feel of her soft touch. It was useless. He had left her. He could not stand up for her. He could not protect their love. He could not save their future. "I ruined our perfect relationship. It's my fault, don't punish yourself.", he had said when he held Sara's hand for the last time.

"As life had other plans for us!", he thought coming back to the present. Their families had ensured that they wouldn't stay together. He tried his best to remember only the beautiful memories of their relationship but the sour words by Sara's family still gave him pain.

He had received a phone call from an unknown number one Sunday morning. The day, for which he planned an exciting date for Sara.

"Hello, is this Dhruv?", an urgent voice inquired over the call.

"Yes, it is. May I know who am I speaking to?", Dhruv had asked casually.

"I'm Sara's brother. Now listen to me carefully, I know what is going on between Sara and you. My family and I don't approve of it. Come and see me in an hour at the address I'm texting you. Don't you dare tell Sara about it.", Sara's brother had ordered, and it didn't seem like he could take a No for an answer.

Dhruv had gulped. His palms were covered in sweat and he felt lost. He and Sara had decided to talk to their respective families about their relationship, but he had never imagined that they would know from elsewhere and would disapprove of it.

He had no option but to obey the stern voice on the call. He had reached the place and waited for somebody to show up. Very anxious, he had moved around to look for Sara's brother. Suddenly, a group of young men had formed a circle around him. "What is this?", he stuttered. "Don't come closer!", he had squeaked as they cornered him. Sara's brother showed up. "You stay away from my sister. We are against these kinds of things. She will marry a boy of our choice. We won't let you taint our family's honour! ", were the most decent lines uttered by him as he abused and bashed him.

He had known Sara's family to be traditional but to be threatened with death was something he could have never imagined.

Sara's brother had made it very clear that Dhruv leaving this relationship was the ideal way to get Sara to agree to get married to a boy of their choice. He had warned Dhruv that he could not tell Sara about it and had to break off their relationship within a few days. Dhruv had returned home after this encounter and wondered whether his parents would have reacted the same way.

After pondering for a while, he had mustered the courage to inform his parents about the situation and seek their guidance on the matter. However, he was shocked when his parents reacted in a similar way.

"Is it because of our different castes?"

"Is it because of the gap in our family wealth and income?"

"Or is it simply because our parents did not get the opportunity to choose our partners?"

He had broken down as he threw questions at his own family, who also wished for him to end his perfect relationship with Sara. Even after a lot of begging and crying, they wouldn't budge. Dhruv had no choice left. He could not abandon his parents and he doubted if he could escape from Sara's family.

The next day, he broke up with her. It was so sudden for Sara, that she thought it was a joke. He was unable to look into her eyes when she shook him and asked him repeatedly on why they were ending it so suddenly. He was speechless. He could not protect his love and nor could he tell her the truth behind it. He was trying to make her life easier.

All these incidents felt as if they had happened just yesterday. They played in his mind on repeat. It was like a movie on the loop that he could not forward to watch only the heart-warming parts. His mind was exhausted, and his heartache grew with every memory and so he pushed his face in his pillow and screamed loudly in agony. In pain. He needed to forget her. He had to move on. "Tomorrow is a big day!", he repeated, finally giving up and drifting off to sleep.

The next day passed in a blur. With so many arrangements to be taken care of, he did not have the time to fall back on his meltdown from the previous night. It was supposed to be his day. As the evening approached, he adorned his newly stitched blue suit, styled his hair the way she always liked and was mentally prepared to take this big step in his life.

Soon, he was standing at the centre of a decorated stage, smiling charmingly at the guests. His bride stood next to him, adorned in her wedding attire as they thanked the guests for being a part of their reception. His eyes scanned the audience from atop the stage, looking for a pair of brown eyes. "Is she here tonight, to be a part of my big day. as she promised she would?", he wondered.

His eyes met Sara's amongst the pool of people waltzing around at the venue. Their eyes locked. She smiled ear to ear, waving and showing him thumbs up along with her husband and his other friends. His heartache doubled. His lips dried. It felt as if everything around him had paused. "Dhruv", his wife, nudged him, pulling him back to reality.

However, he did not miss that tiny tear rolling down from the corner of Sara's eyes!

26

DARLING SUSIE

by Kanchan Hiranandani

Hello David, how are you doing?" called Susan to the young man crossing the road.

"Hey! I am good, what brings you here?"

"We were just on a walk. Hey, Have you met the new member of our family? She's Susie, my little kitten" she said pointing to a white kitten rubbing against her feet.

"Kitten, oh!!! Good! All the best! I too had a cat named Annie. I used to love her so much" he sighed.

"Used to?! Don't you love her now?" she inquired

"She died in an accident. I have to go dear, I'm running late for my classes." he said and hurried off before Susan could respond.

David was an introvert and an only child. He was pursuing MCA from the University of Mumbai and lived in a rented house in an apartment in Bandra East. He had struggled to find a room, no one really rented out houses to bachelors- especially students.

"How can one love this weird animal!" he thought as he walked to the store.

***

Two days later, Susan had come running to his house weeping. She found him in the backyard, planting a row of petunias.

He had raised his head, finding her there a little strange. It was only then he noticed the tears in her eyes.

"I lost her, I couldn't find her anywhere," she cried.

"Whom??" he asked anxiously.

"Susie... she has been missing since last night. She had gone outside after dinner. I thought she would be back soon. After waiting for half an hour, I had become worried and searched for her everywhere but couldn't find her."

"Phew! You got me worried for a moment, Susan... she'd be back... relax." David said getting back to what he was doing.

"No David!! Listen, last week, Mr. Peter's cat went missing and Mr. Samuel's cat went missing and now my Susie. This is erratic. This can't be just a coincidence. I can sense some foul play in it." she said.

"Foul play... are you serious? Who has time for playing foul for your small creature?" he asked incredulously.

"I am planning to file a police complaint," she said.

"Please don't waste your time. They might be having a great time together and will be back soon" he tried to reassure her.

"How can you be so callous? You know how much I loved her, I want her back at any cost" she panicked, crying again.

"I'm sorry... relax... we will wait till tonight, I'm sure they'll return. If not, we will go to the police station together. Will that be okay?" he tried to console her.

"Thanks, David."

That night, David lay down on his bed, lost in thoughts, "Papa and Mama always believed that cats are a bad omen. I wonder why people keep cats as pets and even love them so much."

He hugged his parents' photograph closer as he slowly fell asleep.

His ringing cell phone shattered his sleep.

"Good morning Susan. What happened?" he inquired with a yawn.

"Susie is not back, can you take off and come with me to the police station?" she insisted.

"I have an important lecture today. I am sure." He tried to reason with her.

"Please, you promised me last night," she pleaded, cutting him off.

"Okay, baba. I will come as soon as my class ends." He gave in.

Susan was one of his only friends. Most people kept their distance from him. Sometimes he thought it was because he kept his distance from them. He didn't like the company anyway.

It was a rainy day. Large gravel-grey clouds blanketed the sky. It was as dark as night even at 10 am.

He dialled Susan's number, "It is raining so heavily, can't we go tomorrow?" He requested

"If you don't want to come, it's fine. I can go alone." She shot back angrily.

"Don't get angry. You come to the police station at 12' o'clock, I will come after my class." He had assured her.

Susan had reached the station and waited for nearly an hour for him.

David came in, drenched but smiling.

"Couldn't find a cab," he said, smiling sheepishly.

"I am so sorry for the inconvenience."

"C'mon... you are my only friend Susan. How can I say no to you!"

They went inside the police station and filed a complaint. At first, they were reluctant but on Susan's request, they had filed the FIR. They were indifferent, after all to them it was just a missing cat.

The next day David and Susan had gone again to enquire but they were told that the police couldn't find any clue.

Susan wondered if they even looked for the cat. Even after a week, Susie couldn't be found.

***

Mr. Samuel was an old man in his late sixties. He lived alone and had people over once in a blue moon. He used to joke that he was living his retirement dream, with no worries.

Susan stopped at his house and rang the doorbell. He beamed at her as he opened the door.

She gave him a small smile.

"Hello uncle, I just wanted to know whether you got your lost cat back."

"No beta. We couldn't find her anywhere" he replied sadly.

"Uncle, you should file a complaint too. My Susie is also missing for a week. I had filed a complaint" she informed.

"Oh my... So sad to hear that beta. I will surely file a complaint. I miss her so badly.", he said.

He had adopted his cat a while after moving in. They were inseparable. Susan could see how much it had affected him.

There was no trace of Susie even after two weeks. She had lost all hope and decided to go to the Animal Welfare Society. She requested them for help, claiming a theft. She returned home only after they had assured her that they would look into the matter.

After similar recurring incidents from that area, the police felt pressurized and came around for an investigation. They started inspection from the street where the first complaint was filed. They interrogated many people, they even suspected animal attacks.

Susan was relieved that they had actually started looking for Susie.

A week into the investigation, the patrol dogs had found something unusual in the backyard of a house. Everyone who had filed the complaints was informed about it. Susan was asked to come there immediately.

She was dumbfounded at the sight that met her eyes. The carcasses of eleven cats were found buried in the backyard of David.

Susan had called David and asked him to come home urgently. Something told her not to tell him the reason.

He reached within half an hour.

"What happened?" he inquired.

"We found the carcasses of eleven cats in your backyard. Can you please explain?" asked one khaki-clad officer sternly.

"Carcasses?!! What??? I don't know anything!"

"I doubt you too! I had seen you wandering around late at night, but I didn't know it was for this" the watchman informed the police, looking at David.

He was taken in for further interrogation.

Susan stood there, not knowing what to do.

***

It was revealed later that David had confessed.

Susan rushed to the station, unable to believe what she had heard. She wondered if he was being framed. But, on reaching there, she saw David was sitting in the lockup, with his head resting on his knees.

It required a lot of coaxing to let the officer allow Susan to talk to him.

"David!!" she called out.

He turned to look at her, face devoid of any emotions.

"I don't believe it. You didn't do this, did you?" cried Susan.

David just looked at her vacantly.

"Answer me!"

" It was me." he replied calmly.

"Wh... What? How could you?? How could you kill those poor creatures?" she sobbed, "How could you kill Susie?"

"I hate cats!" his cold voice echoed.

She stared at him blankly.

"I hate cats. I will kill them all! I hate them!" he repeated.

Susan could only stand there, wondering what David was talking about.

David spoke without being prompted.

"It was my birthday night. We were going out for dinner, me, and my parents. We were very excited. Suddenly a cat ran in front of the car and to save it, Papa drove the car into an empty bus on the right. It was saved but I lost them. I have been alone since then. I have nobody now; it was all because of that cat. Papa always said that cats are bad luck. Still, they bought me, Annie. They did everything to keep me happy. I lost them because of that cat. I hate cats. I looked for that cat everywhere, then it had escaped." He continued.

"I killed each and every one of those creatures I saw since then, they don't deserve to live."

Susan couldn't muster the words to respond, yet she managed to do it somehow.

"So, Annie?"

"I killed Annie too." he said.

"Those innocent creatures, it wasn't the cat's fault or Annie's or any of those poor creatures you killed, it's not going to bring your Papa and Mumma back." cried Susan.

David resumed his position in the cell as Susan continued to sob.

The officer, who had been watching their exchange, silently ushered her outside.

***

Susan stood there in the crowded courtroom with the rest of the complainers. She clutched at Mr. Samuel's wrinkled hand, listening to the judge proclaim the sentence, "...... mentally unfit..."

27
SOUR LIFE

by Lalitha Srinivas

He leaned forward, resting his elbows on the table. "Diya, it is okay to open up. It is okay to let go."

It was our fifth session. I had gone there because the guilt was killing me. I had no idea what to do. My husband had no idea that I was in here. He has been supporting me too much already. I can't burden him further with this.

I looked at the nameplate on his table and read his name again : Dr. Vikas Gupta. He looked calm and collected and had a soothing demeanour. He genuinely was trying to help me. Only if I could open up.

"Diya?"

"Huh?"

"It's okay. You can tell me. I'm here to help you, remember?" he said gently.

I took a deep breath and began.

"I have ruined lives. I'm sure there's a place in hell for me. I don't have any peace of mind. I haven't had it for a while now. I really want to get away from this, doctor."

"Whose lives, Diya?

"Karan, I hate him, doctor. I still do, but is it because of me that he'd come to where he is now? And Shrey I don't even know what became of him. He had a bright future ahead, he left it all because of me. Right now, I'm ruining my husband's life too. I'm not able to live peacefully, doctor."

"I'm sure there's a lot more to it, Diya. Why don't we talk about it?"

"Okay. It all started when I met Karan when I was in college. He was my senior. I was not a fan of him at all. He intimidated me all the time. But then, one day, he told me he had fallen in love with me. I regret so many things, doctor. But I regret saying yes to him more than anything. I still have no idea why I had said yes that day.

There began a very sour life.

I thought what we had was love. I had no idea of life and how actual relationships worked. Eventually, Karan showed his true colours. I was confused by his behaviour and second-guessed my decision. I then realised how wrong I had been in ignoring all the red flags - he constantly belittled me, ignored me, and had no regard for my feelings. I wanted to end things with him. I really tried... But he wasn't making it easy for me. I had failed to see his gaslighting and assured myself, 'Maybe things would be better again. He loves me, doesn't he?'

One day, things were too much for me to handle and I ended things with him. Unable to accept rejection, he did everything he could to get back at me. I had no idea what he wanted.

Tactically, he ruined my reputation, one step at a time. Not long after, my friends accused me of cheating on him. He made them believe that he left me because of my infidelity. I was alone, with people talking behind my back. Nobody wanted to talk to me. Nobody wanted to sit with me. Even my professors doubted my character. I couldn't bear it anymore and confronted him. He laughed and told me that more rumours shall follow unless I give him a second chance.

With my college and studies still in tow and not wanting to be all alone, I even thought to give Karan a second chance. Karan continued to harass me. I couldn't let my family know. Though rich, they were very conservative, and it was after a long struggle and because of my best friend Yash that I could come to college in the city. If something reaches their ears, I'd have all my dreams spoilt and married off to some guy I hardly know. So, I put up with it."

I took a deep breath. He gestured for me to continue.

"One day the super seniors called me to give me an official warning. In our college, the super seniors were as powerful as the professors. They dealt with matters of ragging and other student complaints. Anything, before reaching the management, would reach the super seniors. If the issue remains unaddressed, the management intervenes.

My heart was pounding when I was called to the senior's block. I thought someone had let them know of Karan and they were calling to help me. They shattered my hopes when they thrust a complaint a junior had filed on me. I scanned the crisp piece of paper. It read that I had asked him to strip in front of me. I was shell-shocked. I hadn't and would never do such a thing.

One of them finally spoke, "Diya, this is a criminal offence. We can't do anything about it. He has even given his name. Acknowledge the complaint and accept suspension from the management."

I refused to take it in and asked them to accompany me to the said junior. I didn't even know the guy. At the mention of the police complaint, he spilled the beans and confessed that it was Karan who told him to make such an allegation.

I saw red. I screamed at them and challenged them to do something about Karan, who has been harassing me since a long time now, right under their noses.

Though these incidents were darkening my life, I had a silver lining too. Yash. My best friend. We have been friends since childhood. Our parents knew each other too. We went to the same school since childhood. Now, our parents sent us to the same college. My mom always told him to keep an eye on me. He was quirky, fun and above all, he was my constant. We had no secrets. He knew everything about Karan. I had not listened to him when he told me that Karan was abusing me mentally.

I vented about the incident with the super seniors to Yash. He held me as I broke down in tears. The next day, Karan stormed into my classroom. He walked up to my desk. He put his leg on my chair as he warned me to stay away from Yash. "You will regret it if I ever find you talking to him," he said.

Though I was terrified, I acted as if nothing was wrong throughout the day. I refused to let Karan control me. In the evening, as we were heading home, I asked Yash if he had talked to Karan. The sudden change in his expression told me he had. But he refused to say anything. I didn't want to push him further.

Turns out, he had gone to meet Karan and speak on my behalf. And it ended up very badly. The principal was involved, and he had given both Karan and Yash an official warning.

One evening, after college, I was headed to the bus station. As I boarded the bus, I looked for my wallet and phone, both of which were missing. I was stuck, with no way to go home or contact anyone. I borrowed a co- passenger's phone and contacted my mom. I told my mom to call Yash and tell him to meet me at the bus station as I had misplaced my phone and wallet.

Yash met me in five minutes. He immediately felt it was Karan's doing and begged me to let him drop me home. Unbeknownst to us, Karan was watching us leave. It was indeed his plan to get me alone and try his hand once more.

A few days later, rumours of me and Yash began circulating in the college. I could hardly go to the canteen as there would be people there, asking me about it or laughing at me behind my back. With each day came new challenges, new tortures. I began to think of filing a police complaint on him, without my parents knowing.

While Yash was supportive of it, he told me to be wary of my parents' reaction if they came to know. I had lost my peace of mind. I found people in happy relationships around me, I even found happy people who were not in relationships. I had no idea why I had to be miserable.

I stopped speaking and inhaled deeply.

The doctor got up from his chair and walked up to the mini-fridge by his table. He poured out two glasses of orange juice and handed me one as he settled back down.

I took a sip of the juice and it was then I noticed how parched my throat was.

He was gazing at me, waiting for me to continue.

"Shrey joined the college mid-semester. He was a star student - excellent in studies, very kind to all, attractive. He developed feelings for me some time later. I was already in a mess and I was in no way going to acknowledge his feelings, let alone return them.

He hadn't told me anything directly. He had just made it obvious to all by confessing it in one of our free periods to our classmates. He wasn't disturbing me. He would go out of his way to not disturb me or create any trouble for me. Still, I wasn't at ease. I knew Karan would come back from his project tour and it'll be trouble all over again.

Slowly, Shrey tried to take things further. He sent me a message on Facebook, which I ignored. He also tried to talk to me in college.

I tried my best to stay away from him. A part of me began to feel bad.

I told Yash of what was going on. He assured me to follow my heart and he shall take care of the rest. "You deserve to be happy, Diya" was what he said.

I decided to take things as they come and not let a mistake like Karan ruin my happiness.

One day, I saw Shrey watching my seminar from the monitor room. It just made me so nervous, I began to stutter. I had no idea what had gotten into me. He walked out and waited for me to finish my presentation. As I walked out of the room with a few of my good friends, he stopped us and told me he wished to speak to me. I already knew where it was going.

He confessed to liking me. He told me that he doesn't expect me to reciprocate it, but at least not to ignore him. As I was about to speak, I saw Karan standing in the hallway. I rushed back to class, mentally kicking myself in the process. I didn't want to be scared of him, but I was.

Shrey texted me again on Facebook and this time I replied. I told him I had a boyfriend. He had done his share of research and replied to me how he had learnt everything from his friends in college who warned him of Karan. Shrey was persistent and told me how much I mean to him.

Every bad thing that happened with Karan came rushing back. I texted Shrey that I wasn't ready for a relationship and that I could only be a friend to him now.

Surprisingly, Shrey agreed.

The exams were approaching, and things were quiet for a while. Then one day, as me and Yash were in the canteen, one of my friends asked me if I had heard the latest rumour. It had become a habit and we paid no attention to it.

In the midst of all this, Shrey and I talked every single day. I started to develop feelings for him. He had told me he would like to meet my parents after the college year. I was too scared to admit my feelings and I felt it was too soon.

Then one day, there was a commotion in the canteen, and I found Karan dragging Shrey by his collar. I tried to intervene before the fight ensued, but it was too late. Shrey had a black eye and a cut in his lip. Karan screamed like a maniac and shouted at Shrey to stay away from me. This time, he was suspended for two weeks.

Shrey was hospitalised for many days. He had much more injuries than we had seen. I didn't want to put his life in danger. Even after he returned, I avoided him most of the time in college. Luckily, the Arts Fest was approaching, and I was one of the organisers. I had practically no time to eat.

Things were going very smoothly. We had lots of free time, it was colourful, and everyone was having fun during the rehearsals. We were playing cricket in the seminar hall. I had always wanted to bat. Shrey asked if he could bowl for me. I didn't want him to get hurt again. But everyone else convinced me. "It is just one game, Diya! Please!!" they said.

Karan crashed the game and used it as an excuse to attack me with the ball. I had a sprained neck and inflamed shoulder.

I realised I would not be free of Karan, not anytime soon.

"It's here I fear I've made a huge mistake. I told Shrey to leave college. He did. He left everything behind and walked away. I chose the easy way out. Karan continued pursuing me, some days he begged, some days he threatened to kill me, finally he stopped harassing me as I got married to another guy. He killed himself... I..."

I couldn't speak for a while. He waited patiently as I tried to compose myself.

"I couldn't help but feel it's all my fault. Shrey left his hometown, he stopped his studies. He didn't even know I had loved him. He could have had a great life, but I spoiled it. Two lives were ruined because of me." I couldn't control my tears.

Half an hour later

I stepped out of the room and took determined steps home. I kept repeating the words he had told me. Karan's death wasn't my fault. He was disturbed mentally and there was nothing I could've done to stop this. It will take time, but I shall heal.

I reached home and freshened up. I checked my Facebook profile for his account: Shrey Khurana. I sent him a message and the response was immediate. I could convince him to come back and resume his life fairly easily.

If only I had the courage to do it at that time, more often than not, our mind plays the villain in our lives and it's only once in a million times that it turns the tables and reclaims its steps and most of the time, it gets too late, but better late than never.

28

UNREAL LOVE TRUMPS REAL FRIENDSHIP

by Aarti Shahdadpuri

5 June 2020

I received a call from an unknown number. A familiar voice greeted me. "I am getting married, so I thought I should share the news with you." It has been three years since I heard her voice. I missed her. I had imagined myself hanging up the call if at all she called me.

I was shocked for a while but happy for her. A range of emotions churned in me.

I asked, "Who is the lucky guy?"

"Vivek."

I was surprised. "Who is he? Not Karan? You and your mom had planned for him to be your perfect match, right?

"It was our mistake to consider him as the one. He was never trustworthy. I met him a few times, but it was all so meaningless that he ended up not talking to me. He left me as well, right after you. Soon enough mother found me a suitor. I like Vivek, he is mature and good. So, my wedding is on the cards, and you are cordially invited."

It has been three days since the anniversary of three years since we last spoke; we had broken all records of not speaking with each other.

I had wanted nothing to do with her.

I remembered the times when three days of not talking would feel like the peak of being upset and sometimes we could not even resist three hours without talking.

Spending the whole day in college with her and hanging out aimlessly at her place to decide what to do with life, I had lived the best part of my life with her. I had never thought any person could tear me and Muktha apart. We had promised that we would share all our struggles and success. We had wished to grow side by side through thick and thin - achievements and fallouts with men and struggles of being wives, everything.

I thought she knew what she meant to me, that no matter whoever came into my life, she would still hold a special place in my heart. She was afraid to lose me and our bond. She hated if anyone tried to vibe with me more than she did. Such was our friendship. Such the value she held.

I heard her complain all the time about the hypothetical distance which never existed, to begin with, the differences that she felt between us, and the silence that we started sharing. I kept convincing her to change her absurd jealousy towards the new people I met but above all she knew, didn't she?

It was on the cards that her nonsensical behaviour would piss me off one day. So, then there was the day she lost me for good and was left hung and dry.

22nd August 2017

It was her birthday.

I hadn't met her since morning and had lied that I had been caught up and might not be able to make it on time.

I had planned a surprise visit to her place with Amaya.

5:30 PM

She was playing with her younger sister in her bedroom while her mom quietly ushered me and Amaya into the living room. We decorated it with her favourite balloons, gold and grey, and ordered all her favourite dishes online.

Her mom had asked me to invite Karan too (her crush), who was their neighbour, whom she had accepted as her son-in-law since the time she knew. He was unaware of her crush and we thought this would be a good chance to let him know.

I remembered her face blushing, smiling ear to ear throughout the celebrations.

Being fond of Karan's photography, we had reminded him to bring his camera along to click her pictures.

As the celebrations progressed, Karan began clicking my pictures, unbeknownst to me.

I was busy setting up her speakers to play romantic music so that I could make her tick off her secret wish list. The day seemed so perfect, as the utmost reason of all the celebration was to see her happy not because it was her birthday, because she truly deserved to be happy and feel all the love in the world.

The next day when she sent all the pictures, I was furious to see my pictures instead of hers.

What saddened me was the unsaid words which placed themselves between us.

I told her to confront him; he shouldn't have clicked my pictures without consent especially when I had not been familiar to him. The very next day, she had met him in the evening.

When we talked then, I was horrified to see how she had changed. I couldn't believe how a guy could ruin a bond between friends with such ease.

To calm down, I assured myself that we had never given the power to anyone to break us apart and that nothing bad could happen.

It was 5:00 pm, Mukta had gone to meet Karan. After chitchatting for a while, he confessed to her, "I have a crush on Sonya. Sonya's smiling face is something I can't get over. I want to date her."

Mukta was stunned.

Composing herself, she had said, "I know Sonya, she will never say yes to you."

"I bet you, I will impress her within a week."

Later that day, Mukta had called me and told me everything. I got furious listening to his words. I was wondering how a person could think so obscenely.

I had assured Mukta that there is no need to put it in words, but whatever may happen, I wasn't interested in him at all. Neither could I think of dating my best friend's crush.

My words had no effect on her. She had detached herself from me.

We stopped having long conversations. I realised my honest behaviour; my innocence would not help me to make things normal

So, I went to her place in person as I couldn't let our friendship succumb to these misunderstandings.

As I walked into her building and parked my car, I saw Karan passing by and for a moment I was thinking of punching him and never seeing his face ever again.

Composing myself, I stepped towards the stairs

I heard a voice behind me call out, "Hey Sonya, good to see you girl, how are you?"

I looked behind dreading it to be Karan because he stayed in the same building,

I was right. It was Karan. I smiled formally and told him that I was doing fine. Not wanting to talk to him further, I interrupted his pleasantries stating I had something important to do and rushed along the stairs.

He couldn't stop me, so he said "Alright no problem, take care"

As I rang the bell, Mukta greeted me by the door with an unwelcome smile. She went to her room and I followed her. I greeted her mom and hugged her younger sister as always.

Her mom seemed upset with me as if she knew everything which was between us, so she had a small talk with me regarding my whereabouts and health.

After that I rushed to Mukta, she was folding clothes and setting up a cupboard. I helped her with the same and she offered me coffee, which was unfortunately too sweet for intake, but I drank it with no complaints as if I punished myself for the wrongful doing of her prince charming.

Finally, she looked at me and said, "I don't think we are ever going to be the same anymore."

I felt a deep thrust through my heart. I couldn't believe my ears.

She confirmed my worst fears when she said, "I had been a fool to trust you. I think you were plotting against me. You wanted to be with him too. Mom just told me that you were talking to him before meeting me. You weren't even on a date with anyone else all these seven years. What else is there to interpret."

She looked at me hatefully.

I was broken for a girl I trusted and loved who does not believe me anymore.

I had nothing left to say for no explanation will ever make sense to that lovesick fool.

After all her mom had told her this, I wished if she could just hear what the truth was. My eyes welled up, I told her time will speak for itself, for now, I don't deserve to waste my breath over this anymore, I left.

I shut the door and drove home thinking about all the possible things I could have said or done to fix this. My mom asked me, "How come you are back so early today without my reminder calls? All is okay between you and Mukta?"

I looked at her and assured her that it was just a silly catfight and she needn't worry.

Later that night, I decided to walk out without turning back ever.

I texted her,

"Leave me alone,

Never try to talk to me again,

I hope you will understand me someday."

It has been three years since then and it feels like yesterday.

I sat there numb for a minute.

It is the most happening day for anyone, their best friend's marriage.

But everything that happened was hurtful. Though I healed with time passing by as I cannot let go easily. The place where I was disrespected once will never let me breathe at ease. The people who didn't trust me shouldn't witness my grace either. I heard her voice again and suddenly remembered that I was on the phone.

I gave my best wishes and told her I would try to be there, and I had missed her in these 3 years of my life where she had lost me.

How I missed her!

But I'm not going to give in, I may not be the hero here. But I am not the villain either.

29
INTERVIEW OF A WRITER

by Sumeet Doondani

Hello! Namaste! Salaam! Satsriyakal! Good evening everyone!"

The host's booming voice blared through the speakers. It was the much-awaited evening, the youth icon of the year, the much-loved writer who had been sought after all over the world, had agreed to a live session for a much-awaited talk. Channels all around the country and streaming platforms had been notified and were all set to stream the interview live.

The camera panned in on the writer. Black, greasy hair hung over a rugged, charming face with big, deep-set brown eyes, watched the host intently. A scar, shaped like a crescent, gently fading away was displayed just above the right side of his right eyebrow. Though dressed in a simple shirt and trousers, his lean frame seemed to occupy the most space in the room, with an aura of gentleness and warmth.

There was something extraordinary about him, perhaps it's his unfortunate past or perhaps it's simply his personality. Nonetheless, people tend to become his friend, while spreading rumours about him behind his back.

The host continued his blabber in his falsetto, eyeing the guest, and puffing up with pride on being given the opportunity to talk to the great writer and interview him.

"Welcome to the much-awaited talk show. We are here because we believe that human potential is nearly limitless, but we know that having potential is not the same as doing something with it.

Today's guest is one of the greatest thinkers of our generation. He's a multiple-time bestselling author who's written seemingly impossible books in the last year! His books are not only true perennial sellers they've also been translated into five languages. The beauty of his words is such that at his 20s, he has managed to not only create some amazing books that shall be read by and revered by readers all around the world but also could be expected to be adapted into movies and curriculums in language."

The audience filled with zest was clapping joyously and cheering for the simple and straight-faced man standing in front of them.

"As a devoted fan, I'd take up the entire evening to sing his praises, and so I request you all to help me in welcoming the bestselling author of 'Trysts and Twisted Tales Series,' the one and only SJD!!!"

Rounds of applause erupted along with the whistles blowing and the young man bowed to the audience with a bright smile and walked to his seat placed opposite to the host.

"Who knew that such a great thing was written in the charts for such an "introverted attention repellent" as you call yourself like you!", the host continued as he sat down.

"Of course, the first and foremost question is the popular one that you had agreed to answer in our interview. You hadn't revealed anything about yourself till today. We hadn't even seen a picture of yours. We would love to hear about your experiences in life and how you happened to become the most loved author of the year. Of course, not only that, but we'd also like to....." The host continued his speech enthusiastically as the writer began to zone out.

"...lost and misunderstood youth of today", the host's voice declared.

On hearing those words, a sudden rush of thoughts whirled inside the writer's mind whispering "lost and misunderstood" always!

He slipped into his thoughts deeper.

Walking through the streets, looking up for the love; lost and misunderstood, he ended up among the graves of his broken dreams. Dreadful alleys, leached labarums, venomous thoughts, vampiring minds drowned him under his own skinny poison. Betrayed for his own generous acts and helping hand, bullied, and blamed as sineous, was him spending breaths to the devil's own fortress.

He remembered the woman of his dreams, who happened to read a single page of his unfinished story and storm out of the room and his life. He had no way to explain his part or convince her otherwise.

He began to get flashbacks of him, as a child of merely four years, starving, locked up in a room and abused beyond humanity.

A hardcore engineer and doctor of his life working on his ways, earning spirit to wave through the ocean of depressing feels, who somehow manages to relieve oxygen each second. This was the future which he was being pushed into.

The differences of his caretakers had also been manifested as frustrations on him. With no one to turn to or a little bit of love, he was always lost in his own world.

Beaten, locked up in his room, as a child, he had always faced cruel acts of injustice, inequality, and torture both mentally and physically at the very place meant to give him unconditional love.

He had to bear it all, be it whatever, it was a suitable thrashing weapon.

He recalled the moments when he was all alone at times, as a child, full of fear, in a loveless life, deprived and depressed.

The thoughts kept coming to him, in waves, and he allowed himself to revel in them.

He remembered how he wasn't enough, no matter how hard he tried. He longed to go to the stars, far away from the cruel world and be with his mother.

He remembered the evening he met her. The gentle breeze and the setting sun after school. The day he turned to writing as his solace. That evening he was coming back from school alone. He had been walking home and the tiny act of rebellion he did by buying a candy bar from the small old shop.

There, he had met her. She could be seventy. Or maybe even a hundred. Her hair glistened silver and her frail hands shivered slightly as she tried to hold a pen. Being curious, he walked up to the verandah where she was sitting. The dusty paper in which she was writing caught his eye. Her eyes glistened as she wrote, oblivious to the poverty around her.

The young boy had asked her, "What are you writing dadima?" She looked at him quizzically. Her eyes were almost glazed over, white. "This is just something I'm doing to let go of my bad experiences and feelings to be as happy as I'm now" Her gentle smile and the script in the slightly brown paper captured him.

Seeing her smile, he pushed further, "Will I also be able to get rid of my feelings and write like you?"

She was deeply moved. "Of course, you can my child! But may I know what bothers you in this very young age of yours?

He whispered "Nothing Dadima..." and smiled at her. She saw the sudden change in his expression and stroking his head, she uttered, "May God be with you and may the blessings be always upon you."

She was the first person to have talked to him gently.

Maybe the world wasn't all bad, he had thought to himself that night.

As he left for home, he was thinking about what he was going to write and how. He hardly got any time after the chores he had to do.

That day, he found an old diary in a cupboard. His eyes sparkled as he penned down whatever he felt. The first thing he wrote was about the old woman. He wrote describing her wrinkled face, soft smile, and gentle blessings.

After penning them down, he felt his thoughts perturbed as a newer sense of perception arose.

However, however hard he tried; he couldn't bring himself to write. Not the way he wanted.

A few days later, he had loitered around the same verandah, looking for her. She was nowhere to be found. Losing heart, as he began his walk home, his eyes latched on to a crumpled figure on a few sheets of newspaper. He rushed to her, pulling out his dull and faded shirt to offer her some warmth.

She seemed fast asleep, shivering slightly. He tried to wake her up, shaking her. It was then some random passer-by thought that he was trying to steal something. Well, a scrawny little boy in the streets without a shirt was bound to attract attention. Before he knew what was happening, a mob had formed, and with not much ado, they began to thrash him black and blue. He tried to explain how he was trying to help the woman, but it fell on deaf ears.

Finally, the voice of the woman screaming at them to stop hitting a little child brought them to their senses. He had not stopped to look back. He ran away. Away from everything.

A few hours later he had come back and found the newspaper sheets empty. She was gone.

That day he wrote something, pouring his heart out. He started writing like his life depended on it. He held on to his pen, which was more precious to him than life itself. He adopted the name SJD as a mask and with that, he advocated for the change in the world he had always wanted to see.

And a sudden streak of neurons, heart beating out of the chest springing tears in eyes he paused! Deprived of a mother to the stars at an early age was as heart-breaking as separation from the love from life! But, he could say, all this had led up to that single moment. He managed to gather his composure as he was pulled back to reality by the host's voice gently nudging him. As his smile returned to his face, he cleared his throat to answer the questions.

30

THE LOST MERMAID

by Arijit Roy

The Lost Mermaid

Nobody knows about the Raven that perches on the deserted bench in the park thinking of it to be its roost thereby making it more ebony and obsidian. It was not like this earlier, it was a harbinger of love, with feathers all white, but soon it ricocheted off the nature of tidings it carried from the mortal world to the totem and at once all of it turned into glossy black plumes. But it didn't complain neither did it become truculent rather it changed the narration of itself and the perception to the world by holding more wisdom, mental clarity, adaptability, becoming a secret keeper, mystique by nature and weathered. Still, sometimes, the harsh croaks made by it exhibits deep cavil.

The Sclera, The Iris, and the Pupil

Status Quo: Hey! Are you ingesting toxin?

Me: Huh! No, it's the saliva!

SQ: Are you sure?

Me: Yeah, of course! I had taken in a cup of coffee a while ago and is still savouring its taste.

SQ: All the Best. But I've seen you slurping the tonic without any reason!

Me: There are only so many places where I could find my panacea.

Emotional Quotient: Are you losing it all? Don't get the bedlam of insanity to get into you.

Me: Hmm!! Don't give me solace, it's all fabricated.

EQ: Does all the greenery disappear during the night?

Me: It's daytime only but the timer has been preset in darkness!

Cold- and Warm-Blooded Vertebrates

I was resting my dorsum on the wrought iron armless chair doing justice to my present self, doing my layered bob fringes craning my neck backwards into a curt ponytail tied by a multicoloured hairband preparing myself for the ergonomics that has now become a quintessential part of my life.

I adjusted myself again as if to perk myself up that no one can get through that terminator which I'm trying to draw for the day. I resorted to my usual adjuncts like mustering the art of smile and restoring the same from not maximising to the extent that it gets spotted. I pressed the Power button on my phone and resumed with the apps already running in the background from last night, scrolling them all over again to explore some new feed.

A few known faces with unknown identities all clad in a temporal manner suddenly come out of nowhere in flesh and blood reminding myself of the vicinities.

X: "Hey, You! Come Here, has the task assigned to you been done already? Make sure and inform me. Deadline is fast approaching, and the other branches are not lending their help. I will pass on the matter to the respective authorities."

Me: "I have already done all I could do Sir with proper care."

Y: "Hey, Listen! Will you help me with these errands? There isn't anyone else. Sir has told me to ask you."

I silently rather ungraciously took over the task from him, connected the phone with my terminal and stashed it in the drawer left to mine. Soon I signed into my routine of pretentiousness.

SQ: Is that the egregious tunnel that leads to macabre every day?

Me: Huh! No, it's the CCTV!

SQ: Are you sure? But you said you feel awkward as you feel engulfed by the black and white nature of it!

Me: Umm...But it gets offset by the colours on the other side of it!

SQ: Is that an object then?

Me: No, it's a receptor!

SQ: Use Blue then! All the Best.

Justified Indent

I was rubbing the corner of my eyes violently with my spectacles stranded on the desk in front watching my act without showing any solidarity as if I would pluck them off from their sockets when I was halted by a quite familiar muffled voice of someone, "Is it glaring too much Mam? Don't rub like this, rather splash some water, it'll soothe." I didn't budge and said, "Nothing serious, it's dust allergy, it'll be okay, say what are you asking."

He was a lithe lad, supple by nature as it seemed, discernibly modest and who can be a covert operator.

He was the one with whom I can share a throwback to my uncharted past which serves as a testimony to my present self.

He stood as he does regularly, supporting himself against the columns of blank cells that were supposed to be filled up carrying a stack of documents and a meaningful smile to the right of me filling up that little bit of void which was there.

That trash can behind us acted as the metonymy.

The throbbing pain in my temple has now magnified into a pulsating one. I was feeling nauseous, maybe jeopardised by the humdrum that led me to this depression like never before.

As if the varmints of the past were playing in a loop before me and I became all the more aware.

It was a whirlpool of caliginosity inside oozing out of the chalice.

X: "Hey, you! Please come here, there is mail from somewhere that pertains to you."

Me: "I've seen and am doing the needful."

I dragged myself there for no reason sat in front of that living organism who was visible to my eye but incognizant to my sanity. I put my arms to rest on the glass atop of the table shifting it slightly from its position like myself and allowed my mouth to make misadventures.

SQ: Are you hiding something from others?

Me: The caffeine wasn't enough for today, I think.

SQ: Are you thinking of wayfaring to the Mountains again?

Me: Yes, why not? But I have become flat-footed, I think.

SQ: No problem, show some mercy on yourself.

Me: Hoodwinked by sharp angles.

SQ: Don't exert too much pressure on pointed objects for it will not make the surface blunt. All the Best.

Anemones

I was not in a mood to pick up any phone calls neither was I feeling like a monger who could manage something out of nothing. I have locked myself up in an oubliette without any trapdoors. The tethers were retching me, and my eyes were slowly turning bright for the wrong reasons. All the idylls of pansy have now turned into a vast melodrama. All the hippo mouthed promises have been scavenged by the canines of mendacity and devoured by the lust of cynicism.

The Good, the better and the worse

It was as if I was stuffed with camphor in my nostrils waiting for the sublimation to happen. I was lockjawed by too many oases while I forgot it was arid all around. I was feeling like my head had been held tightly and pushed in a pail of water while I was gasping for breath.

Present Indefinite: Hey! Are you the same mermaid I once came across under the ocean?

Me: Yeah! But I don't have the tail now. They have been blown away by the torpedoes of past indefinite.

PI: Who were they?

Me: They were creatures who shapeshifted into werewolves. PI: Are you still battling them?

Me: Nah! But I am struggling with the Past Perfect still.

PI: Hmm...I see, you seem to grovel now like a tortoise without any shell to sheath you.

Past Indefinite: Hey! Is it too black out here or is it just fine?

Me: Listen! Just buzz off and haven't you seen the DND board out there. Now allow me to lament freely.

Pa I: I'm sorry for the situations were against us and you and I had to...

Me: It wasn't enough!! Now stop being anaphoric and don't put asterisks on blanks.

It won't laminate the issue.

Pa I: I thought it was italicised, but it turned out to be rather bold, we both knitted a web where we were short of thread! Bye.

Synecdoche

Love bites were infarcted by now. The serum has gone away with the twigs of nostalgia. The arcade was too full of dross. I was longing for mountains to embrace me all over again with their landforms for I wanted to go out of the via ferratas.

The Rolling Die vs The Tarot Card

Somewhere in the Middle

A couple of girls trying to dissemble themselves from one another unlike the latte placed on the table.

Both were very close pals like two dots of the same colon.

Upper Dot: Something amiss? You seem to be fidgety!

Lower Dot: Don't even mention, I don't want to talk about that!

UD: Okay, you may not but you may reveal it to me anytime. You will feel less burdened.

LD: The latte here is worth sipping! I was asphyxiated by the vacuum around me and it felt my head was being minced with shit where I was bageled by the bluntness of the circumstances.

I grabbed up the phone and without giving it a second thought dovetailed the script and how the filmstrip was being cut irrespective of the marquee in the most listless manner as it could get to UD.

Indentured by Obligations with nothing but Aloofness within:

Third Person Singular: Hello! What are you up to? Why are you scrambling on the plate? Eat properly!

Me: Huh! Oh yes.

TPS: Are you not growing up? How many times do I have to tell you to sit properly? And why is the place so messy? Be organised from now on.

Me: I will try.

Woofer With Low Frequency

They say grouping of similar antibodies results in agglutination. It was like a cipher between us where we understood the congruity of the lines we drew.

She: I have a story too!

Me: Is it as gnarled as mine or a few notches of plus-minus is there? She: There are too many recurring decimals between the zero and the one that have confounded my life!

Me: Oh, really! Shake hands, let's be sines and cosines of the same triangle then.

She: Done.

Smooch of Passion

Mountain: Do you love me really? Is it out of amorousness of the passion that has been irked by the downcast heavy heart of yours, I can penetrate?

Me: Err...yea, you may refer to both while one is the marker that summarises the state I'm in whereas the other one is the dropdown arrow that opened without any options.

Mountain: You are fleetingly looking at those crevasses and deep down somewhere trying to figure out a metaphor out of the chasm in your heart.

Me: Aargh! That's prodding...Why don't I even climb up?

Mountain: Yeah! Sure, but make sure to hit the axe properly, and don't look down while trekking, for you, have vertigo. I will be ruthless as ever.

Me: I'm used to it now.

Dialogue between the Cat and the Fish

The cat visited the pond every day to watch its fish, maybe because of some symbiotic relationship they shared between them.

Cat: How are you today? Are you catching up for breath? But you are in the middle of a freshwater lake? Fish: I'm seemingly fine. But my gills are not working!

Cat: Oh! Our situations are the same, we can empathise but cannot swap positions for we may not live otherwise.

Fish: That's the relativity of the food chain.

Cat: Why don't you even blink eyes? You look much better that way? Fish: Oh, really! But my eyes are already moist.

Cat: But you do have scales!

Fish: To hide the grotesque scars. They cannot be lustrated by water.

Cat: Are they too ambiguous to be so unequivocal?

Fish: It's a suitable chiasmus for me.

Cat: It seems you like soldiers and battleships?

Fish: I like how sharpness and precision meet power and brute force.

Cat: Are you trying to be an exorcist?

Fish: No, rather an abattoir.

Cat: May I jump into the water? As long as I can breathe in.

Fish: But make sure I cannot do the same.

Cat: No issues, we are going to just swim together for a while.

Ruffled by the feathers, Hit by the Carpet

The defoliated lights are strewn across the dingy wynds and vennels as if it is chuckling on its own eccentric farce.

The bewildering antinomy of impossibility defenstrates the likelihood of absolution.

She is goldbricking for an echt pretext to express verdancy as the cicatrix of the past is still lush in her background.

The tempest is too vehement to melt away with too little cloudbursts.

Her monosyllabic self is overgrown now that desists her from mincing.

She is trying to form a kiln that is getting ignited thereby hardening her moist soul into a perpetually scathed ceramic.

Maybe the nails are too few to fill the canyons!

The graphics are much more flimsy now.

A tiff between "To and Fro" and "Hither and Yon" that needs to be moderated;

To and Fro: "I am the gladioli of motion that you can ever attain."

Hither and Yon: "Oh really, can you ever be the maximus of moving around freely?"

To and Fro: After giving it a thought "You are not punctilious in your feature."

Hither and Yon: "Even a plain surface is the same but to be a Mesa you have to make it act as an intensifier."

She wonders why and how did this happen to her?

She realises that the drizzle was already there, now the surface that was adorably latent is emerging gradually.

The smudges have now become more discernible than ever.

Maybe it is the passion pit of sandpaper!

The squalor of antiquity is spilling over the froth of virginity.

The Lignin is getting the better of Cellulose now!

The Exasperation of Silence

The rugged stone cobbled by the mud is being reposed, waiting for the high tide to pass away. The ellipsis is now acting as the jargon to the much elaborate and gibberish context. The air is slow on the uptake maybe due to excessive compression. Maybe the grapple was too stiff for it to partake.

Why does she close her eyes?

Well, there are enough reasons for her to keep them open.

Why does she keep her eyes open?

Well, again there are more than enough grounds to do otherwise.

Is that dubiety keeping her at a quandary which she deftly mousses by her savoury ingredients of dissimulation?

Sometimes history needs to be managed by the fullness of time like we trot sideways in order to maintain balance. While she is fidgeting with her "in-between" in her heart that is still true blue to the whereabouts of the mislaid piece!

Snappy Snares

Every oxymoron has their conjunction, every fantasy has their interjection, every abstract has their tangible, we all live in between the paradoxes.

She was still in a state of suspended animation from past memories. She couldn't fathom the depth of the ocean of which she had dived into, but situations made her sail on it with the responsibility of surfing on the waves where she discovered icebergs all around. Alien places and alien people started to torment her both mentally and physically and there was no consensus. The rubble had just settled, and life had just become mundane for us. Every night she used to hear screams and growls from anonymity, and she used to get dissolved in her own misery consuming it as an aberration. It was a dartfish for her to gauge the trajectory of how the ball rolled in which direction. From the depth of abyss to eternity of Zion, from the pitch black of tar to varnished hues, she was cycled by the life of upside down and downside up. The avenues of both convergence and divergence emanated from an analogous genesis.

She tried hard to fill the crevices quite, but she didn't have the idea of what would fit in and she knew that too much shoving would choke her.

MEET THE CO-AUTHORS

Ruchka Gulati

A logophile who pens poems in any genre, Ruchka loves metrical poetry and has written poems in many classical forms. An aesthete and an artist who paints using any medium, watercolour though is her favourite. Most of her paintings have a poem in accompaniment. Through her words, she hopes she can invoke feelings, inspire thoughts, make you smile, reflect, or feel emotions. Her Instagram handle is @wordsadrifting.

Shreya Shenoy

Shreya Shenoy is a budding doctor by profession and a writer by passion. Growing up in a world where everyone is in a race against time, she believes good literature is the panacea for physical and mental exhaustion. She likes to spend time reading and discovering stories regardless of geographic borders or limitations of language. Being an advocate of "simple living and high thinking", she would spend a lifetime educating people about good music, art, and literature to help people elevate their quality of life.

Tulsi Nambiar

Tulsi Nambiar is a tenth grader who loves to read and has always been fascinated with the way you can put ideas into words. She is an avid reader and loves being surrounded by books. This is her first attempt at writing a short story.

Mayuri Kashyap

A girl in her 20's, mostly known as @_agirlwithnojob_ is a writer who is searching for an escape in her writings. She's one of those souls who finds solace in the words which emerge from the bottom of her heart with beautiful metaphors. The underlying beauty is astonishing where she leaves her readers spellbound and coming back for more. Don't miss out her writings.

Aaqilah A J

Aaqilah might seem introverted, but that's only until you get to know her. Having just finished schooling, she aspires to become a pharmaceutical scientist. She was born curious and has never hesitated to take a run at new things. She loves to read and write unique but intriguing stories that showcase an entirely new perspective, and this is her first attempt at getting published.

Aarti Shahdadpuri

She is just a beginner to the World of Writers. She has written her first short story named "The Touch Of Love" in the Anthology of Rehnuma, a poem in "I Owe You One" and a short story "Passion Worth Fighting For" in the book titled "Are We Mere Spectators?" She is currently working with a private firm; her spirit is wild and free. Art is what she feels like. She has run through the fire of hell following in the footsteps of misery. She has seen and experienced everything, but it has never destroyed her best sides. She is an ambivert, listens to many but talks to few. At last, she is a splendid cornucopia of love and emotions.

Ravgun Kaur

Ravgun Kaur is a writer and poet from Amritsar, Punjab. She has been previously published in 'Poetica Vol.2' (by Me Poetry), 'Beautiful ways to say' (by Katie Elizabeth) and 'Field of Hues' (by Writer's Pocket) and can be found as @soul.infused.words on Instagram where she is the editor-in-chief and live  host at 'Untwine Me India'. Her poetry is straight up an expression her own experiences, while she describes her stories as a fusion of imagination and real emotions. When not writing, she can be found talking to the night sky, reading, playing the guitar, singing, or memorising rap music, watching a rom-com, or trying to learn a new language.

Amritha Suryakumar

 Amritha Suryakumar is an avid reader with a fascination for mythologies and fantasy. Her passion for teaching and thirst for conversations steered her towards becoming an English teacher. As a freelance writer, she is keen on exploring different forms of storytelling. She occasionally dabbles in poetry. An unapologetic Chai-addict and self-proclaimed cinephile, she spends most of her free time in pursuit of good Chai, Cinema and Conversations!

Tipston Rubus

Tipston Rubus, hailing from among the natural resplendence of Kanyakumari in India, poetry became his first interest. Once he started sharing his poetry under the penname Tippu, he extended the creative gestures to popular narratives. As a literature major, a befitting calling was in academia, where he imparts the literary passion to emerging young minds at Loyola College, Chennai. Alongside that, his interest in travel, politics, films and food leaves him with an experience that's been nothing short but rewarding.

Uma Bokil

Uma has grown up in the vibrant city life of Pune. This twenty-year-old finds her vibe in the music, books, dogs, and food, but nothing can make her feel the way words do. There's something hidden between the lines that calls out to her, and she aspires to spend her life following the trail to her calling.

Rukma Anil

Rukma Anil has a master's degree in English. She loves to read, listen to music, and occasionally write. She loves translating texts. Another millenial who loves coffee and is a seeker of her existence.

Sanjana Varma

Sanjana Varma is a published poet and blogger. Her anthology of 60 poems titled 'Songs of Spring' was released in 2017. 'Her Expressions', 'Great Indian Anthology' and 'Sour Candy' contains her select poems. She is an avid reader and book reviewer. Currently, she is working as an English teacher in Bangalore. She  wishes to etch herself in the world of literature and bring happiness to her readers.

Lalitha Srinivas

 Born in Andhra Pradesh on 29-11-1994, She has a bachelor's degree in Computer Science from Jawaharlal Nehru Technological University. She has been part of many anthologies as a co-author and has been awarded certifications for her writings in many online competitions. She is a homemaker, attuned to create art, either it's with ink filled in pen on a paper or brush dipped in the paint on a canvas. She is a traveller, who wishes to explore the beauty of India, rejoice different cultures and cuisines. She started writing on Instagram and dedicates it to her late friend who committed suicide. She is inspiring people by interacting with them and understanding their pains, who are on the verge of committing suicide.

Pritha Shyam

Pritha Shyam, 25, is a web content writer having 8 years of experience in the dimension. She is currently residing in Kolkata, West Bengal, and has completed her master's degree in English literature. She has a flair for wordplay, and the passion for writing runs in her veins. A travel freak and a bibliophile, she engrosses in Bengali and English fiction writing in her leisure time. She has also opened a social media page recently named-The Magic Pen and her website is www.munthemagicpen.com. She aspires to be one among the best in the arena of writing.

Sandhra Sunil

If not between the pages of classics or the octaves of her favourite melodies, find Sandhra intently trying to decipher heated political discourses. With undying love for Indian architecture but majors in English literature, it wouldn't be a surprise if she quotes Dostoevsky and Rig Ved on her epitaph, for a paradox she sure is.

Manoj Vaz

They say, everybody, dreams in black and white. Manoj is an award-winning copywriter with 3 decades of experience handling over 50 blue-chip clients. He has published four books; Tinsel - a hard look at Mumbai's Show Biz, The Kidnapping, and the Meth Mystery - both part of the Magic Chest Series for teenagers and Random Musings - a collection of original quotes.

Shrey Sharma

To say who he is would be an Artist. To ask what he is known as is Soul Delusionist! To know who he is, he would say it's what you seek to say out loud. To know what he is called, it's the name he leaves behind.
Shrey Sharma, an automobile engineering dropout, currently pursuing a double B.A. in Eng. and English Honours, respectively. He is a writer, poet, shayar, lyricist, vocalist and an artist who has always believed "Life is nothing more than a delusion!"

Kavya Mithran

Kavya is an engineer and budding writer from Kannur, Kerala. She completed her bachelor's degree in Electronics and Communication Engineering from Government Rajiv Gandhi Institute of Technology, Kottayam and master's from Government Engineering College, Thrissur. She has currently joined Oracle FSS as Associate Consultant. She is very passionate about writing and is also a movie enthusiast. She was an active member of 'Shabdhika', the literary club of her college. For her, writing is a means of connecting hearts and pouring out the feelings and sentiments in a breeze. She has been writing on an Instagram page @appledore_peeks, exploring the human emotions portrayed in movies.

Debajit Deb

Debajit Deb, born on 07 January 1996 in Khowai, Tripura, India has just completed his masters from ICFAI University. He loves to read books of various genres and listings music, and that inspires him to write stories, poems, and novels as well.

Kanchan Hiranandani

Kanchan Hiranandani is a Delhi based entrepreneur, poet, and writer. She is a B.Sc. Chemistry Honours and holds an MBA in HR from Banasthali Vidyapith, Jaipur. She has also worked as a banker. An avid reader, it is her immense love for writing that made her a part of this book.

J. Jerome

J. Jerome is a born writer and started writing at a very early age. He was playing with rhyming words before he even learned about synonyms and antonyms. He wrote his first poem shortly after. He started writing fan fiction in the summer before entering high school. He soon moved to write short stories and

eventually became a regular fiction contributor at www.mythicdomain.com. His free time is spent working on his first novel or playing video games that he is so bad at.

Ar. Jerin Jo Thomas

Ar. Jerin Jo Thomas, principal architect of 3 STORIES DESIGN STUDIO and an art curator, is more into the crafting of neotropical environment sand buildings. Spending almost an entire portion of his time in creating his stories with spaces and textures, he never used to write seriously. Always wrote in Malayalam whenever he used to. Lost & Misunderstood has his first-ever piece in English.

Arijit Roy

Arijit Roy is a distinguished writer who has left his mark as a co-author in diverse anthologies across genres. A prolific word player and a conspicuous observer, he creates tacit text as a medium of expression with aesthetic consideration. His sensual nature of depicting complications juxtaposing calmness with cacophony conjures up selective perceptions.

Arijit graduated from the University of Calcutta with Bachelor of Commerce in Accounts. After obtaining his degree, he pursued a career in Banking. In addition to writing, Arijit also is a voracious reader and an astute audiophile. A published author of the book "Flyleaf" with Your Quote you can reach out to him in different social platforms where he exfoliates himself daily.

Snehal Agarwal

Snehal Agarwal is a 21-year-old chartered accountant from Mumbai. She is talkative, a sitcom fanatic and secretly a nerd. Her stories are a reflection of events commonly occurring around us yet ignored by most. She believes in making a change in society, one day at a time.

Sumeet Doondani

An amateur writer, a graduate in pharmacy, and a self-made entrepreneur in his field of study, Sumeet's hobbies are to read, write and make friends. He also loves to spread motivation, counsels young minds and believes in enjoying both life and music to the fullest. He believes that life is a misery, bizarre secrets lie in the darkest depths, so we are to be wise and kind to all, and live with love and gratitude for all you have.

C.L. Williams

C.L. Williams is an international best-selling author living in central Virginia. He has written several poetry books over the years and recently expanded into fiction with five novellas, one novel, and a frequent contributor to anthologies all around the world. When not writing, C.L. Williams can be found on YouTube sharing books from other independent authors or reading a good book.

INKFEATHERS PUBLISHING

India's Most Author Friendly Publishing House

Stay updated about latest books, anthologies, events, exclusive offers, contests, product giveaways and other things that we do to support authors.

 Inkfeathers Publishing

 @InkfeathersPublishing

 @_Inkfeathers

 @Inkfeathers

 Inkfeathers.com

We'd love to connect with you!